# BAD BLOOD

Also by Bernard Ashley

*The Trouble with Donovan Croft*

*Terry on the Fence*

*All My Men*

*A Kind of Wild Justice*

*Break in the Sun*

(Published by Oxford University Press)


*Dodgem*

*High Pavement Blues*

*Janey*

*Running Scared*

*Dinner Ladies Don't Count* (Blackbird)

*Linda's Lie* (Blackbird)

*Your Guess is as Good as Mine* (Redwing)

(Published by Julia MacRae Books)

# Bernard Ashley

# BAD BLOOD

## Julia MacRae Books

A DIVISION OF WALKER BOOKS

Text © 1988 Bernard Ashley
All rights reserved
First published in Great Britain 1988
by Julia MacRae Books
A division of Walker Books Ltd
87 Vauxhall Walk
London SE11 5HJ

British Library Cataloguing in Publication Data
Ashley, Bernard
Bad blood
I. Title
823'.914  [F]   PZ7
ISBN 0-86203-316-0

Made and printed in Great Britain by
Billings and Sons Ltd. Worcester

*for Evelyn*

# CHAPTER ONE

Ritchie Collins looked at his father in his leathers, at the way his face was sharpened by wearing the helmet, at the way he always became someone else. It was something he never quite got used to; his stomach tightened and some nervous reaction made him look about to see how people stared when the team first went in. Up to that moment it was always candy-floss and hot dogs, the throb of ice-cream vans and the din of old music – a summer fair or fête, another day out for charity. But when the revving began and the sixteen Suzukis were being held back by sixteen men in their tight red, their straight spines and shining bikes waiting to ride the bumpy grass, Ritchie would draw in his breath, and only just stop himself from making a small noise in his throat.

"Not watching, are you?"

Lucy Bowyer had come as well today, sat next to him on the coach but got such a lot of attention from the lads in the team that she'd been turned the other way most of the time. So they hadn't talked enough for her to tell him she didn't want to see her dad ride.

"I *was*... Usually do. What you going to do, then?"

Lucy pulled away from the paling. "There's a castle place over there, and boats. I can't take all this kids' stuff..."

"Kids' stuff?"

"Manly stuff, then." She tossed her head at the people along the fence. "Throwing balls at coconuts, then stuffing themselves with ice-cream while they watch my dad risk breaking his neck."

Ritchie turned, too, put his back to the slow pattern of precision riding going on behind him and looked at the

1

gawping faces. In a minute her dad and his would fly up two ramps at different heights and cross over in the air in a near miss, a dangerous stunt. He could see what she was getting at. They'd really get a kick if it ended in a crash. But wasn't other people's stupid attitudes all the more reason for people who *did* care to stay and watch? He didn't get time to argue it. Lucy's hand had grabbed hold of his and was already pulling him away.

"Boats?" he asked, through a squeeze of backs.

"There's a moat thing."

"A good sailor, I am." And he found himself holding on tight till they were through.

"*Watch now, ladies and gentlemen, boys and girls, as S'arnt Dick Collins and Corporal Eric Bowyer throw their machines in the air and do the flying cross...*" Back in the arena the bikes revved in two corners, ramps were dragged into place, and while the tannoy hummed, the talking stopped in the crowd. With a nod of his helmet, Warrant Officer Sullivan gave the signal and Collins and Bowyer opened up for the first of their jumps.

But from over on the other side of the manor house the engines seemed very remote. Litter on the grass, left-over bunting on the bushes and pedalos on the moat said it wasn't a normal day in the country park. Otherwise the pair of them could have been in an upper-class private garden at any time since the walls went up. The grass was cut in lines, the bushes were undamaged and the trees looked like ancestors. A middle-aged couple trundled a paddle-boat but the rest was still. Tannoy and applause drifted in only faintly and the hot dog smell was going the other way. Out of sight of the fête Lucy had slowed to an aimless saunter, overbalanced a couple of times like someone on a tightrope. Ritchie kicked at clumps, and twisted: both of them walking in keeping with the conversation. They went to the same school, lived in close army quarters, shared fathers' jobs, and yet on their own there seemed to be nothing straightforward to say. Ritchie could think of plenty

2

who would have had her laughing or arguing by now with easy, confident words. But he was always one who went more for his thoughts than for a lot of blab. And a lot of those thoughts right now were about this girl. She'd definitely done something special with her hair today; out here in the country it seemed to have more colour to it, more red. And she'd got it up with a thin dangling ribbon which was asking to be pulled.

She turned her head suddenly and saw him looking. "Funny old castle – with pedalos!"

"And a Norman garage..." Lucy gave the house the eye. Ritchie laughed and lifted his chin, desperately tried to think of a joke to follow it with.

"You ever been out with Tracy Brown?"

"No!"

"She fancies you."

It was like a sudden push in the back. "Eh, what? Never noticed her much." Suddenly he couldn't breathe quite so well nor sound the words loud enough for the open air. What was she going on about, coming out with something like that? He hadn't been asked that sort of question since he'd been in the Juniors. Here she was looking all grown-up and talking like a ten-year-old...

"It's true. Don't you ever think about that sort of thing, eh, Richard Collins?"

"No!" he blustered: but too quickly, and the muscles in his neck wouldn't let him shake his head.

"I bet you don't!" And she burst out laughing. "See your face!" But somehow the laugh wasn't derisory, it was embarrassed, too, in its own way. She'd gone red, and for a moment she was as awkward as he was. "Sorry, Ritch, didn't mean to be stupid..."

"No, I don't mind."

"I just...don't know you, that was all..."

Ritchie stared at her: then he pulled a face. "You ever been out with Pearson?" Pearson was to their school what King Kong had been to New York. And it was just the right

3

thing to say: opened up talk about kids in their class just enough to see them once round the moat and straight back to the arena.

As usual the Red Helmets' long-loader and the team coach were formed up in a vee with the riders' bikes in a long angled line between. At the open end a small circuit of miniature three-wheelers was giving the younger children a thrill. Ritchie's father, in his track-suit and beret again, saw them before they saw him.

"What about that, then, Ritchie?"

"Eh?"

"The ride! What about that idiot Wilkins?"

Ritchie swallowed. What *about* Wilkins? Just because he'd missed it for once, why did Johnny Wilkins have to go and do something different? Had he come off or just gone wrong on one of the manoeuvres? Shit! How could he tell his dad he hadn't stayed to see the ride when that was the reason he always came?

"What *did* happen?" Lucy came to the rescue. "I didn't see."

"*What happened?* Only couldn't get the blessed ladder in! Ran round behind us like the comic interlude!" Dick Collins shook his head in disbelief, which Ritchie imitated. One of the Red Helmets' claims to fame — at least among the rival outfits — was their 'seventeen up' stunt when five bikes circled the arena gathering the men for a pyramid as they went. They ran to catch up, jumped on and clambered up backs till just the last was left, running with a metal ladder which slotted into the centre bike and climbed to make the apex. And it wasn't easy. It was a lot easier to get everyone into position before coming into view, which was what the other display teams did.

"Had 'em laughing their heads off, the berk!" Five years in the team and being second-in-command meant that Dick Collins cared very much. To a real soldier like him, what Private Wilkins had done had been as bad as failing in battle.

4

"Mr Sullivan said anything?"

"Not a lot. But look at his face."

Ritchie looked at where the warrant officer was ignoring some kids hovering near with their programmes. Short and slight with a neat moustache, he could be charming with the wives and children. But right now his expression said it wouldn't be the time to ask him if he'd accept a month's paid leave, let alone give autographs.

"It is bumpy," Ritchie said. "If he missed the first time..."

"You *don't* miss the first time. And it's always bumpy in fields."

Ritchie shut up. Leave it there, he thought. His dad's face was white and tense and he looked tired again. The leaders always got upset when something went wrong, always had a post mortem till blame was laid and something was done to make sure it didn't happen again. They'd have Johnny Wilkins chasing a bike round Thames Reach Common all week, slotting his ladder into those sockets till he was doing it in his dreams.

And why not? Ritchie asked himself. His dad was right. You couldn't set yourself up to be a precision outfit and then do things which had people jeering at you.

"I don't s'pose he meant to miss," Lucy said. "I bet he feels worse than anyone right now."

"So he should." Dick Collins straightened his shoulders and walked off to supervise the loading of the bikes.

Ritchie would have nodded. But not today; and not, somehow, against Lucy. "Cheers!" he said instead, because she had rescued him. "You fancy an ice-cream?"

"If you like..."

And he'd never done that before, either. She smiled, and walked with him. And although they still hadn't much to say, a lot found itself being said. That stupid business up at the castle could have been the end of it, she could have just said no about the ice-cream; but she'd gone with him and she didn't let on she didn't really want one till he'd chosen his.

And she walked round a few stalls with him, and accepted one taste on the way.

"Better go," she said at last. "They'll be off in a bit."

"Yeah. Don't want to get left behind on our own, do we?" It just came out and he coloured up, daren't look at her.

"Worse thing I could ever think of!" she said. "Come on!" And making hurrying excuses she grabbed his hand and pulled him through the crowd again. But this time he didn't let her drop it till they were almost where his dad might see him.

"That was bloody awful! The worst show we've ever put on – and the C-in-C Southern had to be there to see it."

Warrant Officer Sullivan was on his feet next to the driver, the team sitting up in the coach in front of him. They were wearing civvies but their backs were very straight. Definitely army. No-one ever sat up like that in school, and for a roasting there was no way they would be lounging in their seats. Ritchie and Lucy tried to keep out of it, at the rear, half-hidden by the racks of leathers and track-suits.

"It's got sloppy, too much of a good time by half! What some of you need is to get sent back to your units, damned quick! There are plenty who'd give their pay books to be where you lot are!" He pecked at *pay books* like a rook.

Usually the great thing about the coach home was everyone unwinding from the high of the ride, with this man Sullivan laying on a few crates of beer, even getting the singing going. Next to the sharing the different shows with his dad, it was what Ritchie enjoyed most. But the atmosphere was tight and tense today, worse than he'd ever known, even after a bad smash when they'd left a man behind in a local hospital.

"I'm saying no more now." W.O. Sullivan's face was as red as the leathers swaying on their hangers. "It's an o-six-hundred parade tomorrow, machine inspection at o-seven-hundred and a full day of practice till I'm satisfied we dare show our faces at Colchester next week. And don't give me,

'Church parade, sir,' because where you're concerned laddies, I *am* God – and, by God, we're going to put this pantomime right!" He stared them out, and sat down suddenly to light a cigarette – smoking two before the conversations began to get going, regional accents in such low voices that they were hard to understand.

Ritchie peered round the seat in front to look at his dad: was he excused from old Sullivan's rant: were they planning new moves on their magnetic board like they sometimes did on the coach? But Sullivan's arms were folded and he was staring hard through the big windscreen; while Dick Collins' head was lolling on the seat-back, sleeping again. Ritchie frowned: and Lucy had to say something twice about an XLJ which had overtaken them.

"I said I fancy one of those one day."

"More'n ice-cream, then?" He came back to her; suddenly made his inside roll by coming out with something he'd only intended to think. "Don't s'pose you fancy one tomorrow?"

"XLJ or a raspberry ripple?"

"Both if you like. What about going over the park?" He was surprised how calm and flat his voice sounded. Inside, his stomach seemed to be doing what his dad's did flying through the air.

Lucy looked at him with her head on one side as if he was being a bit pushy now. Had he broken some rule, then? All at once he wished he'd stuck to Suzukis and talk of acceleration.

"Our park?"

"Yeah..."

"With all the army kids? Get seen?"

"I don't mind getting seen." And he didn't. He'd never been flash and all over the girls like a lot he knew: swearing at them and all that business, treating them rough. Instead he'd been the opposite, kept himself much more to himself. But he wouldn't want to hide going out with this new Lucy.

"Me neither." She laughed and leant into him. "I'll drop a

7

card through Tracy Brown's door!" She was looking at him now as if he'd passed some test. "No, see you over Greenwich, by the statue, top of the hill." She patted his hand. "Bit less hassle."

"Yeah, whatever..." He widened his eyes at her and suddenly felt so good he really didn't know what to say. He couldn't go back to how nice the scenery was. And then it was her hair which gave him the line. "You gonna wear that ribbon?"

"It's only old..."

"I like it."

"I'll wash an' iron it, then."

And all the rest of the way home Ritchie didn't go back to thinking about his father and the team, not even when Dick was talking about their bad day on the walk from the coach. He felt detached: a bit like the first time he'd crossed the road without help.

And he slept well. He'd always had the knack of going off as soon as his head hit the pillow, and even a whole new dimension to his world didn't seem to make any difference. It was a gift he wouldn't appreciate having till he lost it later. As it turned out, it was the waking up next morning which was so different. Ritchie normally took each day as it came, never made a fuss about getting-up-and-going, school day or weekend. All that suddenly changed, because what hit him now was the very special feel of waking to this new sort of friendship, a curling of the toes and a lightness in the legs which left him floating on the mattress as if he were filled with bubbles; shivering him as he thought about the girl. And for once, instead of getting up, he wanted to stay there, to go over the signs from the day before, to wallow in all the doubts; he wanted to lie there in a comfortable stew and question what different things had meant, ask himself whether she hadn't been friendly like that just because he'd been the one there; and feel jealous of the blokes in the team who'd had a smile from her. All the time hanging on to his ace – keeping the thought close to his

chest and bringing it out like a winner every few minutes –
that it was *him* who was meeting her in Greenwich Park. He
tried to think about Lucy herself, to anticipate the afternoon: but the peculiar thing was, he couldn't get her face
back in his head. He could conjure up some of her, her red
hair and that ribbon; he could hear the sound of her laugh;
and, feeling very pleased none of his mates could see, he
could squeeze his own hand under the covers and pretend it
was hers. But as for getting her to look at him again and
smile, somehow that was impossible. He'd have to wait for
that till they actually met.

He turned over on his front, spread himself out as if he
were climbing a cliff and enjoyed the feel of having someone
special to think about. His head on one side showed him the
clock. Poor old Dad! He'd been out three hours. Well, this
was better than stripping down a Suzuki and riding round
Thames Reach Common...

"Ritchie Collins! Ritchie! You making a move? Toast's
getting cold."

Toast? *Toast!* So his mum was up, then. Well, the last
thought in his head this morning was about toast – especially
that charcoal she served up. But he moved: knowing her,
she'd be in his room with a wet flannel if he didn't make
tracks. She was like that – cup of cold water, put the cat on
his face – a good laugh first and think about it later. There
was nothing for it but to get up. She'd definitely done for
any more thinking about Lucy Bowyer.

Within ten minutes he was looking at his mother through
the door jamb to see what sort of a mood she was in. He
and Lucy hadn't been very secret about saying cheerio and
"See-you-tomorrow", and though he knew his dad would
never say anything about it to *him* – nothing as embarrassing as that – he could well have told his mum in bed last
night. So was she waiting for him ready to hum 'Love Story'
when he walked in the room, or to make some pun on
Lucy's name? Because that'd be her mark, all straight face
and big eyes, with him starting to go red and then going

9

even redder trying to stop. But his first impression was that she looked a bit quiet this morning, thoughtful, doing the crossword over a mug of her atrocious coffee; jeans and v-neck jumper, hair all brushed. No, she wouldn't give him a bad time, he reckoned. She'd got something else on her mind. All the same, he went in very carefully, like an actor going on the set.

"Feel sorry for Dad," he threw in. "That idiot Wilkins! Bet there's a few of the lads blessing him!"

"You can say that again! He needed a good lie-in, your dad. The alarm nearly went up in smoke before he came round and turned it off."

Ritchie scraped some butter over the tile of toast, looked at his mother; the sharp one of the family with the cross-word nearly done, the pretty June with her long dark hair and brown eyes. It was rare to hear her feeling sorry for his dad – usually she was geeing him up in one sort of way or another.

Doing a clue with her right hand, she poured his coffee with her left. Ritchie was as quietly proud of her brain as he was of his dad's riding skills and rank. Sometimes, looking in a mirror and seeing her colour eyes in his own, and his dad's thick hair, he hoped he'd got a good mix of the two of them, all the way through, all the right genes: the best of her side and the best of his. His dad came out of the army next year and one of the team sponsors – the helmet people – were helping to set him up in a small motorcycle repair shop with a helmet agency on the A22 near Godstone. With his mechanical skill and the business brain his mother was wasting on her receptionist job with Barry August Products, they could make a real go of it: and with motorbikes in Ritchie's own blood, he might even have gifts of his own to help him pull his weight. Now he looked at her, chewing her lips with white teeth, thinking. Beauty and brains and a lot of fun, for a mother.

"Now –" she clicked her teeth with the Bic – "a four-letter word meaning 'makes you feel special' . . ."

Ritchie frowned, tried to think.

"Begins with 'L'..."

"Don't ask me. 'Love'? No..."

"'Alternative meaning –'" but now he knew she definitely wasn't reading it out of the paper, her smile said she was making it up, "'young and beautiful'!" And here she trilled it up in the air till she spluttered her coffee all over the paper.

"You...!" Ritchie was torn between going for her and slamming out of the room.

"Now – 'Hit a tender spot'..."

"Dunno what's up with you! Nothing to make a big thing about! Stupid!" He pushed out to the kitchen to find some cereal. She *was* stupid, too, he thought, making him embarrassed about something normal.

From the kitchen window of their flat he could see the back of Hussar House, the block where Lucy lived. It was a good job she couldn't hear this rubbish, that was all.

"Sorry, love. Don't mind me. She's a nice girl. Nothing wrong in a bit of...romance..." She'd come up behind him and put a hand on his shoulder: but she couldn't miss rolling the 'r' in 'romance'. He could get very cross very quick if she didn't watch out. He concentrated on dealing with the cornflakes. Couldn't she understand that he could just do without all this nonsense, that with her it only made him wriggle inside his skin?

He gave up, scooped some spilled cornflakes back into the packet; wasn't in the mood for eating. "What time's dinner? I'm going out this afternoon."

"When you like. Snack. I'll cook tonight when Dad's here – if he'll eat it."

Ritchie went. She'd annoyed him, gone too far with embarrassing him. She didn't know where to draw the line, that was her trouble. And even while he tried to get a bit of homework out of the way, he could hear her across in the living room singing: "Love is a many splendour'd thing..." Probably not on purpose, but it was what was on her mind.

11

Well, love might be all that, he thought: but you had to give it half a chance.

"My old grandmother could look more dangerous with her vacuum cleaner! She could command more attention getting biscuit crumbs off her carpet!"

A night's sleep hadn't done anything for George Sullivan except perhaps sharpen the cutting edge between his tongue and his teeth. His small blue eyes shone and his trimmed mouth issued lethal words with all the velocity of automatic fire. The twenty-nine men who made up the squad were lying on the grass at the edge of the parade ground, sucking short stems, their ankles crossed, shoulders heavy on their elbows; but still they had the stiff necks of attention. Dick Collins stood eyeing the lads next to the warrant officer, nodding along with what he was saying, while the number three, Eric Bowyer, crouched alone with a rag and a spark plug.

"We've got twenty-three more shows this summer, three big County Days, two swanky Tattoos and a load of week-end fêtes: and I'll tell you, when they don't go home in their motors talking about the Red Helmets then *we have been wasting our time!* The oil people won't sponsor and Suzuki will start looking for someone else to give their bikes to. Do I make myself clear?" He suddenly pivoted on his left foot to face the one man who was sitting up cross-legged. "So what do you do, Private Wilkins, if you miss the slot with that ladder? You stop, and stand to attention, and wait for the formation to come round again. You make it look *difficult* – not some bloody Keystone Cops turn-out!"

"Yes, sir."

"All right." He turned to the others. "And kindly remember, in the cross-overs, we're supposed to have them holding their breath when we make for those gaps. Not give 'em time to go to the beer tent and back! Ye gods, the room you're leaving yourselves I could take a Churchill tank through! I want sixty m.p.h, not fifty – and I want you aiming at those back wheels, not thin air. I want people not *daring* to watch. Not, not *bothering* to watch!"

There was a mumble of assent. They didn't argue. They took it because they were army and he was of superior rank; also because they were in a showy unit and they reckoned themselves to be the cream; but most of all because they knew that not only was he right but that anything he wanted from them he would cheerfully do himself. This rare sarcastic moan was coming completely out of character from a man who'd much sooner be out there leading them astride his bike.

"Right, then, get at it. Sequence nine, from two corners – and don't go from all four till I say so. Clark and Brentwood lead; Downing, take my place and Heale and Baker take S'arnt Collins' and Corporal Bowyer's. Get at it and you might be done by lights out!"

Looking energetic the riders sprang up.

"Dick, Eric – I want a word."

The long, elegant façade of offices on the further side of the parade ground began reverberating with Suzuki crackle as the zp 400's were kicked and throttled, the blue machines and the red quickly forming into two eight-man lines. Sullivan and the other two N.C.O.'s, helmets still off, stood and watched them.

"And I want something a bit nearer the mark from you two," Mr Sullivan said quietly. "And from me. The lads only follow the standards we set."

Silently the three of them watched as the crosses began, faster and tighter this time. There were more acceleration roars and brake squeals and swervings at first; but the gaps were certainly getting smaller and the old twist of danger just under control began to come back to the display.

"I'll take them onto the Common for some more of this on the grass. You two can work on your cross-over with the ramps." Mr Sullivan stopped, as if he were wondering how to put it. "Eric, you're ducking your head, man. I could fly Concorde between the pair of you." He was putting it very

13

bluntly; but only because he would do their ride himself. "Bring your height down, Dick, save air space for the car jump; aim for passing Eric behind his back, where he's just been." He screwed his face, smiled, enthusiasm winning over against any criticism. "What I want is, we give it all the makings of a collision in the air, right up to the second when it isn't. There's no point doing it, otherwise." He looked at Eric Bowyer, whose attention went back to his spark plug, and at Dick Collins, who was forcing his tired eyes to focus. "All right, Dick? Not keeping you up, am I?"

"Sorry, George. No, I've got you." Ritchie's dad turned to Lucy's, forced himself. "What we'll do, we take it as before, only instead of both our front wheels hitting the ramps together, I'll hit mine with my front wheel as you hit yours with your back – and I'll pitch mine lower, too. That way we'll miss in the air by the distance between two wheels." Eric Bowyer still said nothing. "Get the timing right first by doing it side by side with the two ramps parallel."

"First class." Mr Sullivan slapped his leathers with his gauntlets. "I'll bring the lads back in an hour and we'll show 'em something, eh? Gee 'em up! Only I'm not having this outfit laughed at, I tell you. I'll pack it in 'fore I'll do that."

It could have been a more private meeting for Ritchie's first with a girl: but a Sunday in early summer is never the time to aim at being alone in Greenwich Park. Crowds in light clothing wander all over like litter and the squirrels join in everything. The consolation is that with so much young love draped on each other's shoulders – like the French students who come to London and suddenly discover one another – there's nothing remarkable in sideways smiles and the holding of hands in a royal park.

When Ritchie had arrived, his first worry had been actually finding Lucy among so many people. Sunday in Greenwich wasn't his scene, and he hadn't reckoned on the crowds. But there she'd been on the steps of the General Wolfe statue, looking cool and lovely in full white cotton,

14

with the ribbon done up another way in her hair: and the guts inside him had given a flip and he'd felt sorry for everyone in the world that day who wasn't Ritchie Collins.

"Wotcha!" He put on a swaying run up to her and took in the busy scene. "We pulled the world and his wife today, then!"

"Or the world and her boy-friend!"

"Yeah." They laughed; stared at one another and the question of a greeting kiss hung in the air; but it didn't get a bold enough answer; just a cough. "Where d'you want to go?"

Lucy shrugged. "Don't mind. Somewhere a bit quieter?" That part of the park overlooking the Thames and Christopher Wren's classic architecture had certainly attracted people to it. Cameras blinked as often as eyelids and there were smiles enough to save the world as people posed with feet each side of the meridian line, then queued to shuffle between the telescopes and the timepieces of the old Observatory.

Ritchie and Lucy went. And quickly picking up from the day before, they held hands at first; then taking encouragement from the French, within metres Ritchie had draped an arm over Lucy's shoulder and left her the natural option to hold him round the waist.

It was a first for him, and of course he didn't know about her: but would a squeeze ever feel the same again? And would words ever rise beyond grunts in the throat? Words somehow didn't come into it much at first. Slowly, going away from the tourist attractions, they wandered off into longer grass and lonelier trees. A bit at a time, though, and nonchalantly they swapped tales of their backgrounds: schools in Germany or Hong Kong, in Wiltshire or Essex and a brief spell for Lucy in Northern Ireland: but never anywhere together, it seemed, till this latest posting to the display team based in Thames Reach. And what they couldn't understand was how they hadn't even noticed each other in their time at the comprehensive.

15

"I just thought you were good at Maths and drank your orange a bit quick," Ritchie told her.

"Best thing about you was your calculator." They sat down on a slope facing Greenwich Power Station. "So how would you sum me up now?" she suddenly asked him.

"Pretty...ugly! Jumble sale clothes. Boring. Smelly feet..." He'd closed his eyes and was lying back. "A pain to be with. What about me?"

"Oh, I don't know..." There was a silence, leaving out the cars and an aeroplane and some distant screams. He squinted to see her still on an elbow thinking up some insults of her own. "Hair too short on the top; but nice brown eyes; nose a bit on the long side but it wouldn't do any shorter; a little moustache coming..." and now she traced a finger tip along it; "...a nice mouth, specially when you smile; not too pushy." Another silence. "Someone it's nice to be with..."

Again Ritchie's back lay light as air, and inside him was a weird mixture of excitement and calm as if he were in some different dimension of living to ordinary people. If he'd fallen from a high building he'd have survived, because the normal rules of life had been changed for him that day. He couldn't remember anyone saying anything so good to him ever before. And he'd chickened out from being anywhere near nice to her...

So he kissed her. He hadn't planned it as such and he didn't know it would happen just then. But without any sort of warning he put a hand on her shoulder and pressed her mouth with his lips: and at the touch she went away from him, and he went with her, very confident that she wouldn't make him feel a fool. Quite the opposite. There was an electric moment as their tongues first touched and then it was all noises in the throat and a closeness like deep sleep as they lay on the slope and didn't notice the sun go in. Afterwards, the long kiss and the hard holding over, Ritchie still found it difficult to say anything special enough: words definitely didn't come to match the magic of all that: and he

16

was more sure of himself on safer ground.

"See that power station over there?"

"Couldn't miss it, could you?" Lucy shook bits of grass from her hair.

"See those four chimneys on the corners?"

"One, two, three, four," she counted. "Correct."

"Someone said one of those was built false. They only needed three but they built four for show."

"You learn something every day!"

"It was my dad said it, but my mother said it was Battersea. Same shape. They kept a balance for the look of it."

"Thanks for telling me. I needed something to remember about today."

"Then someone on the box said it wasn't true anyway. Funny old world, rumours..."

"Funny old world, full stop!" Lucy pulled him to his feet and after various pieces of grass has been returned to the ground they went off to queue for some tea.

"*Unfair* old world!" she suddenly said. "Making our dads do an extra day's work when everyone else is doing this." Ritchie looked round him at all the sauntering in the sun; nodded, but said nothing. "Sullivan's got no right. He doesn't *own* them!"

They'd got to the cafeteria by then and Ritchie was relieved: because he didn't really agree with Lucy and yet he didn't want to argue with her. Being in the army meant doing as you were told. If an officer said you'd got to do something to get it better, then you did it, no questions – Saturday, Sunday, midnight or Christmas. If you didn't like the sort of job it was, you didn't do it. But who wanted an argument with someone who made you feel as terrific as she did? He gave her hand a squeeze to compensate for his thoughts. Well, her dad was a professional – he'd know, Ritchie reckoned.

"Wonder what school'll be like tomorrow!" Lucy was pushing sugar round the tabletop, and smiling.

"My face'll be red as a beetroot all day!" Ritchie could

already feel the different place it was going to be.

"I won't embarrass you, Ritch. I promise." She looked at him, serious eyes, smiling mouth. "No blowing kisses in Assembly!"

"It'd cheer it up a bit." Now his finger chased the sugar. "But I don't mind...you know..." What he wanted to say was, she didn't have to keep it secret. He'd be proud. He could even think of a few faces he'd like to see: Tony's for one; a best mate, but always showing off about his way with girls. On an impulse he looked at his hands, but the ring on his finger had been his grandad's; he felt at his wrist, but his watch was a cheap garage job and no beauty. Then he went to his neck, to the silver chain and the St. Christopher he'd bought himself once on a day trip somewhere. With a duck of his head it was off and going round Lucy's neck instead. "Now see how long 'fore someone notices," he said.

Lucy smiled, lifted the little disc to look at it, tucked it into her top. And hand in hand, with Ritchie filing away this happiness for later, they went out of the park, past the bus stop and walked the longest way home.

Over on the parade ground Mr Sullivan was looking more his old self. His face bore the expression of a man whose dog would get a good run that evening. The others were sweating and their bikes were caked again, but the work-out up on the Common had tightened the ride to a standard he could begin to accept. He patted his leathers for the cigarettes which weren't there. But seeing the sign the riders knew they'd done enough.

"Not bad," he said. "Better. At least we've got something to work on."

They stood in small groups and looked out at the tarmac. In the middle of the square, two ramps had been set at ninety degrees to each other. One gave a low trajectory, the other something steeper. At the nearer perimeter Dick Collins and Eric Bowyer sat astride their Suzukis, resting their engines and their forearms for a moment. Not long now. This demonstration, Mr Sullivan had said, and they could call it a day.

"Right, now give your attention to what S'arnt Collins and Corporal Bowyer have been doing. And give it a good eye, now, because we'll be talking understudies tomorrow."

"Long as it ain't undertakers!" It was the first dare at a joke since the day before, and from one of the youngest of them.

"You watch this, laddie. This'll wipe the smile off your face, I'll tell you!"

The short laugh ended in looks around. In front of them Collins and Bowyer slid their helmets over and tightened the straps. Again the sergeant's face changed to that other, professional look: that sharpening up. His eyes were focussed and a very tired man suddenly looked a keen soldier. Waiting for eye contact he nodded at Bowyer. Both men kicked their machines and took them off in wide arcs round the men, on the trimmed grass and off it onto the tarmac. As they went they opened their throttles to a fuller throat and made a sweep round the ramps in a dummy pass to come full circle and position themselves in line, fifty metres away.

Set like the hands of a clock at twenty-to-four the ramps were still pitched with one slightly lower than the other. Every man's eyes were on one or the other of them, the watching figures grouped like a very still life. With a sudden jump forward the bikes went, black rubber marking the ground at the eight and the four, machines in such a thrust that they were at sixty in no time, heading inwards towards the ramps and each other, their riders shooting looks across to judge relative speeds and positions against the flags they'd set at the perimeter. Full throttle they went for the ramps: twenty metres, ten metres, one metre in a blink. And even to the team it seemed to be a certain collision. Going that close at one another one bike needed to be much higher to clear – or at least half a metre back to leave room for a safe miss.

19

The ramps clattered under the hit of the bikes, Bowyer's a fraction before Collins', then a split second on the steel and one was flying with the other flying at him. A woman in a window screamed. Men on the grass swore or closed their eyes. But Dick Collins, too low to have missed Bowyer's body, was high enough and late enough to fly behind the other man's back and over his rear wheel, brushing him with a boot, and just missing the mid-air collision. It was the closest thing going.

"Christ!" The men on the grass said very little through a lot of open mouths. But they were on their feet when the two rode over.

"I'm putting in for a posting out!" someone said. "My laundry bill!" And there were more nods than laughs.

"And that's just what we want people thinking!" Mr Sullivan punched his fist into his palm. "We're not putting on good-natured displays like the police lads – we scare the living daylights out of 'em!"

"We scare the living daylights out of us!"

Collins and Bowyer had stopped. "Was that your boot on my back?" Eric asked, looking at his leathers over a lowered shoulder.

"Only the one. You can start worrying when it's the both – and me and my bike between them!"

But the corporal didn't look too amused: he definitely wasn't smiling. And a close look at Dick Collins would have shown a face suddenly transparent of skin with different, old man's eyes.

"That's it, then," Mr Sullivan said. "We'll call it a day."

"We'll call it a nightmare!" Eric Bowyer corrected: but no-one else heard him. The rest were kicking to go. Only Dick Collins was stationary, and he was intent on gripping his bike hard, suddenly having to fight for the strength to hold it upright.

# CHAPTER TWO

It was nearly as bad as changing schools. Being army, Ritchie was very used to turning up outside different head-teachers' doors, very used to all the sideways looks and the testings the other kids always gave you. He hated it: but there was nothing he could do about it, it was just one of the facts of army life. Doing it so often had taught him some of the tricks, of course: like, not letting on how good you were in goal till you found out how big the best goalie was, that sort of thing; and when someone first hit you, you hit back a hell of a lot harder whatever the school rules said, because getting into trouble with the teachers was always favourite over being a push-over in the playground.

This particular Monday, though, he was going to have to face the sneers and grins of people he already knew. And didn't they go potty over finding something to pull faces about? Seeing him go red with Lucy was going to be a real treat for some of them. And how you dealt with a kid being jealous, or with your own jealousy, or with someone being rotten to her – well, he wouldn't know all that till it hap-pened. So, great as seeing Lucy would be, and proud as he was for everyone to know he was going out with her, he still wouldn't be sorry to get this Monday over, thanks very much.

Of course, he might have known the first to show would be Scott Pearson. Pearson was one of those people who couldn't cope with anyone having anything he hadn't got himself – whether it was something to wear or something in his hand or someone to order about: because Pearson didn't really have any friends; they were more like henchmen who'd do what he wanted so long as he had fags to give them, and the other little things you put in your mouth. And right now his supplies were good so he had the power: Ryan and Pickett with muscle he could count on when the mood took him each day.

So Ritchie was in a fair old state – even to wondering what Lucy would do when she saw him: give him a quick wave and stick with her mates; even pretend he didn't exist. . .? He always sank so quickly into having no confidence when he was on his own. But he needn't have worried – she did it perfectly. When he came into the yard she said something quietly to Amarjit and Zo – not a sign of a nudge or a wink – and ran over to him with this brilliant smile. It felt like a bag of sherbert bursting inside him. His eyes went straight for the chain of his St. Christopher which was there round her neck, and for the ribbon, which wasn't in her hair and breaking the school rules but threaded through the top of her blouse. And while he smiled back shyly, he was angry with himself because she'd taken all that trouble for him again, and he'd done nothing special for her, not even found a decent shirt.

"Wotcha!"

"'Lo!"

They stood a good way apart.

"You did well with the ribbon."

"A little bit of brains. You know – where there's a will there's a way!"

There wasn't a lot else to be said just then. School was a tough and public place of rough talk and loud laughs, with no private shade for soft whispers. All Ritchie wanted to do was just get on with the day in the same room as Lucy. A smile now and then would be enough, or the odd word. They could find real things to talk about after school. But he knew there wasn't much in school that went the way he wanted. People like Pearson saw to that.

"Oi – oi! It's bleedin' Romeno 'n Julia!" Pearson was snorting from his corner behind a drain pipe, with Ryan and Pickett like Mafia looking over their huddled shoulders at them. It always amazed Ritchie that anyone ever learned anything with a trio like that in the tutor group.

He definitely wasn't going to run; but he wasn't going to face them out either. He stood where he was and tried a sardonic film hero smile at Lucy. "Think we must've got seen somewhere."

"They were outside the off licence yesterday. Leave 'em."

"Too right. Leave 'em." Without going too quickly they tried a drift away from trouble: Ritchie relieved that it was only shouts which chased after them.

"You bein' a daredevil like your dad, Collins?"

"Bit fast for you, isn't she, son?"

Lucy and Ritchie decided to laugh, just to themselves. "Pathetic idiots!" he said.

But the stupid shouts had raised that other thing which Ritchie had in common with Lucy.

"Has your dad told you what old Sullivan had 'em doing yesterday?" Lucy's tone had changed now they were round the corner; more urgent than Pearson had made her sound.

"No, he went to bed. He was too knackered even to say goodnight."

"Well, you want to ask him, Ritchie." She had stopped walking away and was looking at him with a very serious face. "Honestly. It's not often my dad goes off about anything, but Sullivan's lost his marbles: he's got your dad and mine coming at one another up those ramps like crazy. It's really dangerous."

"I thought that's what they did it for." It just came out, and Ritchie could have bitten off the words as soon as he'd said them. Lucy was looking at him almost as if he were one of those people who'd been lining the fence on Saturday: a gawping ghoul. "I mean, sorry, but..."

"Don't get me wrong, Ritchie: my dad's not a coward!" Lucy's face had reddened in a way that Pearson hadn't caused. "Being brave and being loony are two different things, I reckon. Just because some officer dreams it up for his own glory! Obeying orders without question is..."

23

And Ritchie couldn't finish it, not out loud. . . . *Is being a soldier* was what he wanted to say: what his father would have wanted him to say, he knew. But not to Lucy: not this morning with her in the ribbon and wearing his St. Christopher to please him. "They'll be all right if they're practising an' talking about it . . ."

"It's mad, doing that for a *show*. My dad'd be first in the Falklands. . . But you ask your dad, this new thing's *stupid*. I don't reckon it's macho soldier man to throw one motor bike at another one in the air. For fun. I call that suicide."

Ritchie tried to swing his bag, walk them both on, off this awkward spot. But he didn't get the chance.

"Chewin' you up, is she, Collins? They're like that, women." Pearson and his two had come round the corner and up on either side of them.

"Clear off, will you?" Ritchie had been too involved in weighing his words with Lucy to do the same with Pearson, and it could have been a mistake. For a second Pearson's eyes said he was deciding whether he'd take that sort of talk — but just as he gave the nod for the kill, Des Banks, the deputy head, came striding into the yard to sort out some other trouble. Like a conditioned rat, Pearson pulled away with just one terse, animal word. Because everyone took notice of Des Banks: whether they were sixth form, kids being suspended, their parents, or the head teacher. He was a big man in the Henry the Eighth mould, light on his feet and stylish in a three-piece suit. As he came through the yard his approaching stare had Pearson and friends sullenly turning; and the same look took in Ritchie and Lucy together, with a little dip of his head doing for a page of notes on what he'd seen.

Ritchie, with a Pearson pulse still running, looked up to heaven. "Oh God, he'll give it out in Assembly . . ."

"What?" Lucy asked. "Anyhow, I'll see you later."

The buzzer had gone and they walked in to Registration. But if Ritchie had felt up in the air before, he didn't know where he was now. What a stupid state to be in: having to

24

choose his words, even *control* the way he felt about things. You couldn't run an army on wooden guns, and you couldn't run a dangerous display team on easy stunts. But you also couldn't run a new thing with someone like Lucy on a load of disagreement. Blast it! Why couldn't life be more straightforward?

He walked into the tutor room and found he had to make a quick decision about where to sit. There weren't any regular places. Different teachers liked you in different seats in their own rooms, but in here with Mrs Ross you went where you liked. Which had never been a problem before: somewhere near Sunil or Gerry gave Ritchie plenty of options and put nobody's nose out of joint. With the other mate from the junior school, Tony, they expected to be close to whichever girl he was trying to impress; but Ritchie knew who'd be making a new move today.

In four strides he made a quick bid for an empty double halfway down, then threw himself into one of the seats and slapped his plastic carrier on the table beside him. Why not? he thought. Lucy had worn his St. Christopher and gone to a lot of trouble with the ribbon. They hadn't discussed it out yesterday, but she'd want to sit next to him all right.

Even as he was setting his face to stare everyone out, ready for the remarks, Lucy came in like shy royalty – and went walking on past him down the aisle to sit with Zo. As she went she trailed a hand across his table top and touched his arm. It wasn't the same, though, and it left him feeling a fool, and having to work out a quick slide across to Sunil. But no chance. Before he could make it Pearson and the others kicked their way in and Mrs Ross stood up and started counting them off. "Anyone seen Thompkins or Young?"

No-one heard: last night, tonight and *EastEnders* were all more interesting than where dilks like Thompkins and Young had got to, and Ritchie was on the point of swallowing his disappointment by edging for a chat with someone, anyone, when the room quietened like a three-pin plug being pulled on it.

Des Banks had walked in. The dark suit filled the doorway and the eyes surveyed the room from behind red framed glasses; bringing an instant stillness in a manner much copied but rarely achieved, because this was *him*, and not some act.

"Eileen," he said to Mrs Ross, "I've got a new customer for you." The voice was neither acted up for the kids nor lowered for secrecy, a simple piece of plain dealing. "Sadie O'Connell. Her father's been posted in to the New Millbank."

Poor kid! Ritchie shifted to see the girl behind the man. The New Millbank was the large military hospital next to the garrison; you had to feel sorry when some other army person got thrown in all among the rabble.

"In from Germany."

Mr Banks was well into the room now and the new girl had come in to stand beside him.

The name sounded Irish, but she didn't look it: she was dark-haired with white skin and a Chinese shape to her eyes: and she seemed pretty calm under all the stares, Ritchie reckoned, standing there with her canvas bag against her knees, looking straight back at everyone. He knew about these terrible moments, and he had to admire her. Not many adults ever found themselves in situations like this; and it definitely wasn't easy when nine teachers out of ten didn't want another kid in their class anyway.

And now even Des Banks wasn't above making cobblers of it. As he gave Mrs Ross the admission slip he looked round the room and spotted the empty place all convenient next to Ritchie.

"Ritchie Collins is a civilised man," he said, "*and* he's stood where you're standing, in his time. He'll see you safely to French." All the heads turned for the wrong reason now while Sadie O'Connell was given her instructions about presenting her Day Book to each new teacher she met. Groaning to himself, Ritchie lowered his head and got halfway round to an eyes-to-heaven at Lucy; but he decided it'd make him look too much of a kid so he swung back: and by then the new girl was coming over to him, with Galloways suddenly in for selling a crate of medicine, going by the coughing which had started: and Ritchie cursed again for God making blushing part of the show-up. What he wanted most of all, though, was for Mr Banks to stay: because people treated one another o.k. when he was around – already he'd stopped the coughing with a look – but when he went wouldn't it start again, and quick? To survive it Ritchie would have to be so off-hand with this girl, it'd leave him feeling really bad.

Meanwhile, she had slid herself in next to him and taken out the new Day Book; and after a rummage in her bag she found a pen and started to write her name on the cover. The class was still quiet because Des Banks had stayed to talk shop to Eileen Ross, and while everyone started looking out homework Ritchie glanced at what the girl was doing. Carefully she wrote her name in black italic. *Sadiee O'Connell.* Only when she sat back to let it dry did she spot the mistake.

"'Course, I'm not nervous!" she whispered. "Only petrified!" She crossed out the last 'e'. "And they wanted to call me Angharad except the Hong Kong registrar couldn't spell it!" She looked round at him. He smiled back but said nothing: and the next he saw was a message written on the page of her Day Book and passed under his eyes. *Is this the deaf unit or something?*

Lucy or not, Ritchie couldn't ignore that. "No," he said, "sorry."

"Oh, that's good news!" She took back her book, and in leaning for it she put her head next to his; just for a split second. Apple shampoo, it was, not at all like the special smell of Lucy's. But now it was Ritchie who had the little cough, who shifted his chair and tried to make a bit more room for himself. He pulled out a French vocabulary list, turned half a shoulder on the new girl, and thanked God when Mr Banks went and he could lead the rush for the back row of desks in French.

But the day didn't improve: nothing good happened – and he wasn't a bit surprised. Things often went like that. If one good thing happened on a day, then lots did: but give a day an iffy start and things went on being iffy – and the harder you tried to make things better, the more mess you ended up treading into the carpet. He left Lucy alone, just smiled at her, gave her the eye when he got the chance, but he didn't save her a seat any more. And as for Sadie – she had to look after herself, whatever Des Banks had said; and anyway, she didn't seem short on front, looked as if she'd survive. He tucked himself in again with Sunil, Tony and Gerry and went for a few laughs: but even the old crowd seemed different today, somehow.

He told himself there was a fair chance going home would be different, though, and he made his wrist ache twisting for four o'clock to come. All this school hassle he could take, with the prospect of Lucy at the end of it.

At last the time came. The buzzer went, they banged their lockers shut and, trying not to seem to, Ritchie watched her walk out of the building. But he didn't rush. In that testing way special friendships go, he was holding his breath on what she would want to do.

She waited for him, round the corner outside the gate. Casually, he walked: inside he was running the hundred metres. "You going home my way?" he asked her.

"I'd better be!" And as if the day hadn't interrupted at all, she laughed and held his hand, and Ritchie felt better again. So what a day it had been! Pearson and everything; and how about him getting landed with that Sadie O'Connell, the new girl? "Should've seen your face, Ritchie! Beetroot wasn't in it!" "Even went wrong on her name!" They swung arms and smiled and put their heads together now and then. And the grim day just past meant they did a lot of laughing now, too. It was back to Saturday at the fête and Sunday in the park, the way things were meant to be, just the two of them. And especially when they took the long quiet walk

28

home between gorse bushes and through knee-length grass, cutting across a wild corner of Thames Reach Common. In a spot secluded from everything, except the insects and air traffic heading in for Heathrow, they slowed to a stop and found the grass, the way they had in Greenwich Park. Only now there was no coy conversation, no descriptions of one another: on their own, away from the pressures, Ritchie just wanted that closeness you couldn't ever have in public, to be away from the rest of the world for five minutes. They kissed again, less fiercely than before, entwining themselves, with Lucy saying his name on no voice at all, just breath, and his teeth tingling in his head.

It turned chilly. After a while they began to hear the aeroplanes going over again and they sat up. When out of nowhere, in a very soft voice, Lucy murmured, "Ritchie... I love..." Her words were so quiet they were almost drowned by the sounds of birds in the bushes, and Ritchie seemed to feel the blood draining from his head. He leaned closer till their hair tangled, and now he wished a Tristar out of the sky. "I love...my dad," she came out with, "and I'm all worried about him, Ritchie, I've got these bad feelings..."

Ritchie's face showed concern: but he suddenly felt the way he had when she'd walked on past him in the tutor room. He stood up slowly and pulled Lucy up. He busily dusted stalks away while she asked him, "Ritchie, your dad's got more rank: can't he have a go at Sullivan, eh? Please! That stupid new thing they're doing...my dad wouldn't talk about it if it wasn't, but, honest, he reckons it's crazy..."

Ritchie's hands had got hot and sweaty. He wiped them on his sleeve before he held hers again, began to walk. But he didn't know what to say, and definitely not how to begin.

"It only needs your dad to say something, too. He listens to him..."

"Could be..." Ritchie found. "Only I don't know what it's about myself yet..."

"Will you ask him to stop it? For me? Ritchie?" She had stopped them walking again, but quite unlike before. "If you like me that much?" Her eyes went back to the clearing they'd just left. "Even if you don't *want* to ask him... Will you?"

"You know how much I like you..." He squeezed her hand, hard, knew he was giving the impression he'd do what she wanted. But he wouldn't say so. "Here, what was all that about Tracy Brown, Saturday?" Although he knew very well. She was another army girl who was going to Berlin in a month or so, was just an excuse to get things on a personal level. Lucy only smiled, distantly: her mind on her father? "Good runner, Tracy Brown was. Beat you to that tree!" He let go and ran to a silver birch about fifteen metres away: anything to try to lose the awkward subject: but Lucy only walked and he was left feeling like a little kid. Even a kiss goodbye in the stare of the army flats didn't alter that.

When he got indoors his father was lounging in an armchair in front of a John Wayne video. Playing a soldier with an ankle broken in the Normandy landings, Wayne was getting one of his men to lace his boot tighter for support so that he could go on to win the war. Ritchie laughed. They'd seen the video before and had a good crack at this bit. But this afternoon his dad didn't join in, and when Ritchie looked closer he saw that he was deeply asleep in the chair, mouth open and no frown upon his face. So he left the man in peace and tried to get on with his homework. An impossible job; all he could think about was Lucy, and the kissing, and the St. Christopher where it lay, dismissing the subject of the display ride. Somehow all that seemed totally out of order now he was back indoors with the man. But he was ready to say honestly that he didn't have a chance. Well, his dad was asleep. Besides, give it another day, a few more rehearsals, and Lucy's father might stop whining about it...

*     *     *

Unfortunately, time ran out on all of them. Over on Thames Reach Common the next morning Dick Collins ran his bike hard into Eric Bowyer's in a piece of poor riding, and the bad accident Lucy had feared had happened. To those watching, it was simply as if an aircraft had failed to gain enough height for take-off and had hit what it hadn't cleared. To those involved there was nothing they could do about it. It happened. It was in a timed rehearsal of the show for Colchester when Dick Collins sent his bike at the ramp in the new finale and just didn't lift it off high enough. It was as if the strength to do it was missing. Instead of flying above it, the front wheel of his Suzuki hit the back wheel of Eric Bowyer's and in a wild roar of engines both men and both machines crashed to the grass beyond the ramps. It was a good job they hadn't been on tarmac. Wheels, limbs and red helmets cartwheeled in a screech of engine and then a sudden stillness hit. No movement, no sound: again, just the birds, and the low hum of London's eternal traffic for background. But hardly had the tangle landed, looking obscenely wrong huddled there on the ground, than W.O. Sullivan was calmly giving his orders.

"Piper – you to the hospital for an ambulance. Butcher, come with me: the rest stand firm." He and Butcher revved across the grass to the accident while Piper made off behind them to the modern New Millbank less than half a mile away.

There was no panic. Everyone knew that certain sorts of stunting accidents look a lot worse than they really are. They involve people who are half-way ready for things to happen, alert riders who can throw themselves into prac- tised rolls, because risks taken by them are risks prepared for: like in the long jump over fourteen men who lie down with their fleshy backsides in line with the jumping bike: the worst you get from those light machines are bruised cheeks, but it all seems very dangerous. What looks as if it would kill in the street is often no more than a dusting off of grass in an arena.

31

Even so, it was a few moments before Bowyer moved: and Collins went on lying very still.

"My bloody shoulder..." Bowyer moaned. He tried to pull himself up. "Here, Dick! Dick..."

By now Mr Sullivan and Private Butcher were there: Butcher, one of the men with first aid training. "He's out," he said, his gauntlets off and fingers feeling for a pulse at the sergeant's neck. "We won't move this one. Breathing's o.k." He scrambled over to Bowyer, gingerly felt the man's legs under a barrage of swearing and looked at the angle of the man's right shoulder and arm. "Reckon you've had a bust-up here, Eric."

"Yeah! Great, eh?" Lucy's father looked up at Mr Sullivan. "You see what happened? 'Cos I'll be buggered if I know."

Mr Sullivan was very matter-of-fact. "Dick caught your back wheel: came at you a foot too low."

"Prat! Is he all right?"

"He's breathing."

"Thank Christ for that."

And with that everything had been said that needed saying and all they had to do was wait there till the medics came.

That afternoon found Ritchie and his mother sitting side by side in Dick Collins' bed-space, leaning their heads to catch what the man was saying.

"I don't know why it happened. I just felt weak, went dizzy...didn't make it somehow..."

"But you're all right?" June nodded across two beds at where Eric Bowyer was sitting up in a neck and shoulder harness. "They've not gift-wrapped you."

Dick moved his head in a shake and Ritchie looked up again to stare at Lucy's back. He didn't know how he felt. A sort of tearing feeling inside for the girl, who had walked in with her mother seeming not to have seen him, and an uncomfortable mix of concern and shame for his dad,

32

who'd definitely caused the accident. Plus the throaty choke of knowing that he had been warned about this happening – and had done nothing to help stop it, not even when Lucy had really put it to him strong. What he wanted to do now was get up and walk down the ward to talk to her, tell her he hadn't really had the chance; but his dad looked like death, and he was saying something to them...

"They looked at all the bruising, thought I must have a bad fracture. See, I'm black, blue and yellow all down this side. But going by the x-rays I'm all right..."

"Dick Collins, you used to bruise when I just looked at you!" June told him. "Talk about tender. But what do they expect? You must've come down with a wallop. Here, let's have a look..."

Inside, Ritchie felt bruised and very tender, too; while his mouth ached with the smiling at his dad who looked so ill and at his mum being ever so bright.

"They took some...blood...to check."

Without wanting to turn his head too far Ritchie grabbed a look at Lucy. Her straight back, the angle of her neck and that beautiful hair turned his inside over like a long drop down: and even while his father was talking to them all he could hear in his head was his own name, the way she'd said it on the Common the day before. Half a week ago he wouldn't have been in a state like this. As far as he was concerned her dad and his would have had an accident rehearsing a difficult stunt and it would all have been down to the job they did. He'd have felt rotten for his dad, but there was no way he'd have been all churned up like this. Mr Sullivan would have had his say and he and Lucy Bowyer would have got on with being the different people they were: after all, no-one was dead, were they? But now, knowing how she felt about the stunt, and the way he felt about her, everything was all so complicated and uncertain.

A certain side of which was about to end, signalled by a move down at the other bed. Lucy and her mother got up and kissed Eric Bowyer, the girl giving him a long wave and the sort of smile Ritchie was starting to need like food. Half backwards, half forwards and still twisting they came walking past where Ritchie was. More than anything in the world Ritchie wanted that little classroom look which Lucy had perfected: the flashed stare, too quick for interception: because he needed to be told that everything was all right, really. Underneath. What had happened had been an accident. But Mrs Bowyer suddenly turned towards the door and hammered past on heavy heels, her eyes very firmly on where she was going; while Lucy hung back for a last wave to her dad, then looked to be following till she stopped at Ritchie's shoulder to put the question to him straight. "Did you even ask him?" she wanted to know.

Ritchie half got up. This did need talking about. He did need to explain this to her. "Lucy, I never got a chance," he said. "See, I . . ."

But she had taken a step back, got something from her pocket, held it out for him in a closed hand. He laid flat a palm and it curled down onto it, heavy and cold: his St. Christopher on its chain.

"I thought we trusted each other," she said. "You can have this back." And in a couple of steps she had caught up with her mother and left the ward door swinging wildly.

It was like an attack on the stomach from some spirit hand, something that hurt without the force of a blow but which seemed to grab around inside. The St. Christopher was numb on his palm and his face felt cold. He had to swallow hard as he fought against it.

"Never mind, Ritchie." June patted his hand. "'The course of true love ne'er ran smooth.' Bill Shakespeare."

Dick Collins looked bewildered. "What's all that about?" he asked, fighting to keep his eyes open.

"Nothing," they said together, but the man was too tired to pursue it. For Ritchie, too, that nothing was something too devastating to get to grips with yet, just an emptiness he could already feel when the M.O. came in.

He was a tall man with a lieutenant colonel's crowns on

his epaulettes and an authoritative smile. "Well now, Sergeant Collins," he said, "I think we want a closer look at you..."

"Not recommended!" June said, standing up. But her face was taut, the voice a wobble.

"Yes, your platelet count's a bit on the low side, so we're going to have a little look at your bone marrow. Take a sample from your sternum..." He tapped the centre of his own chest making a hearty, hollow sound. "Just a small injection, a bit uncomfortable, nothing more..."

By now Ritchie was on his feet, too, drawn up automatically in the way a senior officer always draws up an army man.

"Tomorrow?" June asked.

"Why not now? Strike while the iron's hot and then chat about it tomorrow." The M.O. was too relaxed and friendly, and Ritchie in his right mind would have known there was something wrong. But all he wanted was to go – and it was more in the hope of catching up with Lucy than with leaving the medics to get on with helping his dad.

"We'll get home, then," he said to June: and in the way people are when they're in some sort of turmoil, he was all feet and chair legs as he got his mother away. It was only when they got out of the hospital and there was no sign of Lucy that he realised he'd hardly said a proper goodbye to his dad.

It was a thought which immediately shamed him into being strong. What *was* he thinking of, taking a dive over a girl he'd been out with twice when there could be something seriously wrong with his dad? How could he have sat there in the ward mourning over her when the M.O. was going on about blood counts and bone marrow? Ritchie shuddered the unthinkable away. This was his *dad*: and, anyway, he'd get back to Lucy: he couldn't believe she'd say his name like that on the Common and then just chuck him for good the next day...

35

So, stop it! he told himself, finding for the first time that a thought about all that side of things could quickly be controlled by a thought about his dad. For a start, and as a penance for spending too long wrapping the St. Christopher in tissue, Ritchie forced the M.O.'s conversation back into his head; and when his mother was in the bathroom he secretly looked up *platelet* and *blood count* in the encyclopaedia. But it wasn't that sort of book, and there was no-one to phone to ask, nor to tell, either. For some reason they'd never kept in touch with the Collins family – his dad had gone into the army young and never talked about them – while Ritchie's grandparents on his mother's side would only have fretted three times a day for news. So he just kept faith with his dad by jollying his mother along and acting normal: as normal as anyone could who'd had the taste of honey and lost it, and whose father they were all being bright about.

He'd gone into school a couple of mornings with his blood bubbling like Coke; anxious, but with it coming from being special, and very happy. Now on the third morning he was going in tired and flat. Everything that had excited him – a sight of Lucy, a smile, a look, the pain of seeing her say something to another boy – was going to bring him down from now on. And where talking to Tony or Sunil had been second best, now it was all he had again. Back to being one of the lads.

But his twistings in the night had ended up with him determined not to try a persuasion job on Lucy; not today: not till his dad was out of the wood. Although that wouldn't stop his heart rate going up when he saw her; nor his inside churning when he was treated like any other kid in the class she didn't know very well. His only answer was to use his secret weapon and wonder what was wrong with his dad.

And it was someone *he* didn't know very well, the new girl, Sadie O'Connell, who gave him the shock of an answer.

"Sorry about your dad," she said to him in the school

36

corridor, waiting to go in for computer studies. "My dad's on that ward. He told me."

Ritchie remembered how Des Banks had said her father had been posted in to the New Millbank.

"What's he – a nurse?" He guessed he wouldn't be an M.O: only Other Ranks' children came to this comprehensive school, officers' went to Archbishop's.

She nodded: "Ward Ten –" said it quietly and seriously as if it meant something. "He specialises, that's why they flew him over."

"No, wrong one, my dad's on Ward Six." A display team accident would always be the talk of the hospital canteen but Ritchie reckoned she could easily have got the names muddled, being so new. She was one of those confident people like his mum who took on the world before it took her over. Right now, though, she'd stopped and put a hand to her mouth suddenly like a kid who's let a family secret out of the bag. "You good at computer studies?" she asked. And she'd changed the subject about as smartly as Ritchie running for that silver birch the other day.

"Not much. Rather play *Space Invaders*. But what's this Ward Ten your dad's on?"

"Ward Ten?" She started bluffing in an airy and dismissive way, just for a few seconds; but gave up and in a very quiet voice, "Ward Ten is oncology," she said, "where they cure a lot of cancers…"

It was one of those moments when the rest of the world doesn't exist, and Ritchie heard himself saying, "Yeah? Did they move my dad last night?"

Sadie nodded. She squeezed his arm. "Thought you knew or I wouldn't have said anything. God, my dad'll kill me…"

The queue, like a wave let into the computer room, washed past Ritchie as he clung to the wall like a tired swimmer. But Sadie stayed outside with him, even after someone had shut the door on them with a bang. "Probably just testing. And it's not what it was, my dad says. Cancer. He comes home very cheerful. There's tons of hope. Really..."

Later, Ritchie realised that he'd taken the news the way people take the news of a close death: formally, politely, thanking the teller; and with this strange sense of bodily calm. Enough to ready him for his mother's tears when he got in from school, when they could cry them out together. And by the time the two of them got back to the hospital he was raring to fight his dad's disease alongside him. Everyone said cancer could be beaten, he told his mother: well then, the Collinses were going to do it, no question of that!

"It was the tremendous bruising without the break," the M.O. told them round Dick Collins' bed. "And it ties in with your tiredness, Sergeant, and your generally anaemic state. Dizzy spells, some bleeding from your gums, perhaps?" Ritchie's father nodded his bathroom secret: but already he had that soldier's gleam back in his eye. "No wonder you couldn't lift that bike so well..."

No-one else said anything, not even a defiant joke. The only person any of them wanted to hear from was the M.O: Colonel Blake's were the words for hanging onto right now.

"Thirty years ago I'd have told you next to nothing about what you've got; privately given you six weeks to live. Twenty years ago I'd have been in the business of suppressing the disease for as long as I could and improving the quality of what life you had left: but now there's genuine hope and we even talk about it in front of the kids." He smiled at Ritchie. "Big kids, that is. No, there's a lot we can do to cure it these days; and we need the patient's active co-operation as a member of the team which is working to get him well."

Dick Collins pulled himself up the bed a bit. June smiled bravely. And Ritchie couldn't help thinking how sorry Lucy would feel for them all when she knew.

"Now I'll tell you what you've got and how we're going to fight it." Colonel Blake sat back in his chair and rested his hands behind his head, as easy now as a professor with a group of students. "Leukaemia. Literally, *white blood*.

38

Acute Myeloid leukaemia to be precise. Through some abnormality the white cells in your blood are multiplying too fast, aren't being kept within bounds, they're affecting your spleen and your immune system is upset. So we need to get the balance right again. Now we do that first of all with drugs, get what we call a remission, then when your blood's back to normal we move in on the bone marrow where the stuff is made and replace it with marrow which will grow good from then on..."

Put like that it sounded very straightforward. "Right, we'll take the cure!" June said brightly, rubbing her hands. "Barclaycard or Access?"

Everyone laughed.

"It's certainly easier to describe than to do: and I won't pretend it doesn't have its hairy moments. Sometimes we fight it with drugs on their own; chemotherapy; transplants aren't the only answer..." He looked June in the eye. "But there are indications here that a transplant is our best course. Mind you, re-infection – ordinary common-or-garden bugs – are the big enemy when the patient's resistance is as low as it needs to be to start again. And it's uncomfortable –" he turned directly to Ritchie's dad – "you'll lose your appetite and some of your hair; you'll feel low-spirited at times and very alone in the isolation ward for several weeks; but we have a good success rate if we can transplant your bone marrow, and I'll tell you, there are plenty of soldiers doing their duty in different parts of the world who've sat up in that bed and heard this speech..."

Ritchie's throat had tightened. He still couldn't believe he was sitting listening to all this. It was like a film, and in some mad way he'd become part of it.

But what was that about *transplant*? "He can have my bone marrow," he said. "Can I give him mine?"

"Oh, we'll come to all that. I'm afraid you're only a half-match at best. But I'll be talking to your mother about relatives in a bit. Meanwhile" – Colonel Blake stood up, uncoiled himself the way tall people do – "we'll let this chap get back to sleep. He's into isolation tomorrow, has to treat the rest of us as if we've got the plague for six to eight weeks." He dropped his voice, became solicitous. "I'm afraid it'll be at least six weeks before you kiss him good-night again: so I'm off to my room and I'll see you when you're ready, Mrs Collins."

He went from the ward as if he had a lot to attend to but Ritchie heard him starting up an idle chat about the cricket score somewhere outside the door. Slowly, he got up himself and touched his father on the arm. That, too, would be the last for a long time. He kissed him on the forehead, went for a hug but drew back in case he bruised him – this man who'd always beaten him in every wrestle. And he cried, and his nose ran. "See you tomorrow," he said.

"You bet. See you tomorrow, son."

And while his mother stayed behind for her own au revoir, Ritchie went right outside to let some cool air dry his face.

# CHAPTER THREE

"So whose bone marrow will he get?"

By talking about it on their way home they were trying to put a focus on their fears, to control them in some way. Already, Ritchie and his mother had decided it was a good thing the accident had happened when it had, with the hospital being so alert. Better than being on leave in Corfu! Time was crucial and time had been saved. But Ritchie needed to know how quickly they could get the next stage set up and ready to go.

June drove her nippy little Fiat one-handed in the heavy stream of traffic, making points between the gear changes with the other. "There's three options," she said, "Dad's own bone marrow..."

"Eh? How, if his is bad? I don't get it..."

June waved her arm confidently, rattled her bracelets as she swerved past a road works. "They take the marrow out when he's better, in remission; they kill off the bad cells and then they put it back..." Ritchie looked at her. She was always on top, even in the way she answered her phone at work: "Barry August Products," as if she owned the firm. But she was on top most of all when she was driving her car. He could tell she would soon be the western world's greatest expert on his father's illness. "... But that's too new yet to know the success rate." She could easily have been a hospital secretary speaking, putting things in a way he'd understand.

"So what's next, then?"

"Someone else's. Not a relation." June went down through the gears for a pedestrian crossing. "But someone who matches."

"And?"

The car picked up speed again. "Hold on. The chances aren't bad, he reckons. Well worth a go, if they can get the match..."

"*If*... Come on, Mum: you don't look like Mrs Confident..."

"No, really." She flashed a smile at a bare-chested lorry driver who'd let her through. He leant down from his cab to shout something. Ritchie held on tight as the car swerved expertly to let another Fiat edge into a parking space outside some shops; after which the road was fairly clear.

"But that's not the best chance, is it?"

"It might be for us. They've got thousands of donors on their list. Because the other option is...someone like a sister who matches. And there we could well be stuck."

"But there are some. He has got sisters somewhere, hasn't he?" They weren't talked about but there were some, he knew.

"That's no guarantee they match. We'll have to see." She twisted the wheel hard to the right and roared the car away: and Ritchie knew she was holding her breath. If she'd been thinking of saying any more she'd bitten on it: and he knew better than to press her any more. But why only *sisters*? Cutting out brothers wasn't very scientific, was it?

And why that sudden clamming up on relatives? It made Ritchie look up then, in the car, and it worried at him overnight. That, and the knowledge that while he'd still been asleep his dad had gone into isolation and had his first injection; all mixed up with a very real dream of Lucy Bowyer which didn't do him any good. And with it all still going round in his head in the bathroom, he cut a stupid spot having one of his rare shaves.

And that demanded his immediate attention. Didn't blood run free from places near your mouth? It'd ooze a bit from under your chin or on your cheek, but start bleeding buckets from a place where it hurt. He dabbed at the blood with a piece of toilet paper; tried to get it to stick there and congeal

– a glob of good, healthy-looking red stuff like one of the art room inks. Like ink, but so filled with complications, he thought, it was a wonder so many people turned out to have it normal. He grabbed at a Dettol bottle and put some on his face. No, he'd never treat a drop of blood the same casual way again.

He heard his mother banging about at the telephone table, sorting something before she went off to tell her people at Barry August. He was so used to being alone with her in the flat, he never actually *missed* his dad. Army kids didn't. The Red Helmets weren't only a display team – they had to be good shots, good at signals and good at Arctic warfare. In a war they'd be part of a crack N.A.T.O. force, and every year they disappeared for mountain training somewhere: two years before they'd done a spell in Ireland, so he was well used to being the man and bolting windows and dreading the sight of the Chaplain.

And now his dad could die some other way; people did, even with blood looking bright red like his own. What a terrible thought!

He tightened at the unthinkable and in a fit of just having to do something he rushed to throw the cover over his bed before his mother had to tell him.

Like a stupid kid he'd had his St. Christopher under his pillow. He scooped it away into a drawer. Lucy Bowyer! He was only ever a stomach roll away from thinking about her: and he always felt guilty when he did, because the terrible thing was, in spite of all his attempts, she was still the one he really thought about most of all. Those private times in the park and on the Common – well, he couldn't just wipe them out: and even now he caught himself planning that talk which would put things right between them. About how ill his dad was, and how he hadn't had a chance to say a thing. He pictured the chewed lip and the pitying look in her eyes. And he saw her taking the St. Christopher into her hand and putting it back round her neck with a quiet smile. God, what a rotten son for a man to have! What had his dad done to deserve a selfish, self-centred kid like him? Violently, Ritchie ripped the paper off his lip and let his spot bleed: because for one shaming second he'd even imagined her tears at seeing him walk into the school wearing a black tie...

When he really walked into school an hour later it was obvious that Lucy didn't know any of the bad news: and the way she stuck to Amarjit and Zo, it wasn't going to be easy getting close enough to tell her, either. Even if he'd known how any more. Because he saw her smile at a joke of Tony's and it suddenly set him right back.

But Pearson happened next and the question never arose; the pig Pearson who thought a day wasn't right till someone had spilt tears or blood somewhere on the school floor.

Lucy hadn't come into the tutor room yet when Sadie came over to Ritchie and quietly asked after his dad, a close, caring enquiry, sweet breath and kind eyes. Ritchie told her his news, thanked her politely with a smile.

Then it was the word from Pearson and the laugh like someone flushing the bog.

"Wassup with Collins? Goin' over to chinkies, are you, Collins? 'Ere, let's know if they're any diff'rent!"

What people said was true. At first you didn't believe your ears. It wasn't meant to be more than quick-sprayed graffiti from Pearson, and already he was pushing on to upset someone else; but the words hit Ritchie in the face, and he could see the hurt for the new girl.

"You great dick-head!" Ritchie twisted himself round on Pearson: wanted to hit him in the mouth but did it with the words. "Why don't you keep your pig filth to yourself?"

"Oi!" Pearson had stopped. Already he was loving this, the pleasure of what would have to come; smiling and looking round. Ryan and Pickett pushed over a couple of chairs in their way. "Oh dear, Collins!" Pearson took off the Michael Caine glasses he wore...and slid them straight back on again as something told him a teacher had come. "See you later, son!" he said. "*See you later!*"

Those were the words from him which caused kids to be off school for days, crying to their mums with imaginary pains. But somehow Ritchie didn't care: it was weird, but he just wasn't scared. Life was treating him badly enough: what more was a beating up?

He soon found out. They jumped him at first break, and went too far, as they usually did. Ritchie had gone outside to the yard to stand his ground, ignored all his mates in his martyred mood, deliberately evaded them and found himself a place by the parked staff cars on the tennis court: not the place to go to hide – it was where the smokers went – and not a chicken run like the library or outside the staff room windows: but there was grass, a patch with a small hockey pitch where the ground wouldn't hit so hard: and he waited there. Having put himself in for a kicking through what he'd said, he wanted it over with quickly.

But no-one came: the whole break was a nervous non-event, like expecting exam results and the teacher being off sick.

When they jumped him was after the buzzer had gone. He'd seen no sign of them, thought they were leaving it till dinner break when they'd have longer; so he ran in to the lavatories for a quick pee on the way back to class. And there they were, not giving a toss about missing a lesson, banging out of three cubicles as one, just as he walked in.

And now that it had come, Ritchie swore. This was a long way from the grass, it was all hard sinks and door edges, and there was nowhere to run for the chance of better ground. He stared into Pearson's eyes for the first real time: had never found the need before. And what he saw was a sort of dead hatred, as if the eyes had no living brain to feed back to. Ryan and Pickett were different. One had a sharp eye on the door, the other was actually smiling in some genuinely amused way. But Pearson was a zombie.

And it was too easy, three against one. A sudden run, a push, a skid on the piss and Ritchie was over, trying to scramble for his feet before the first kick came into the side

45

of his head; trying to think fast, moving hands and arms in quick reactions, covering up. *Protect the head and the face!* But boots came in at his spine, at his knees, his kidneys – and when his two hands and two arms weren't enough to give protection any more, they came back at his head.

Not a long job: and without a lot of noise: Ritchie not landing a single blow in retaliation, not even a lucky one. Suddenly it just went quiet, only the automatic flush of the urinal sounding loud enough for Ritchie to risk a look up. And they'd gone: left him behind with his blood and snot and useless hands, face flat to the filthy floor, legs lying like a road accident. It was even comfortable like that after a fashion – till he moved, and then the ache stiffened into him and it was a painful haul to get near enough to a sink to run water; an even more agonising effort to lift his eyes and dare a look in the soapy mirror.

God, he looked a championship loser at the end of fifteen, just before they got ice on the swelling and lowered the dark glasses. His cheek was all up on the bone and his lip was fat and split, with a swollen nose bleeding buckets of the bright red stuff. It made his cut spot feel really at home.

Shaking in shock, Ritchie washed his face and ran the cold water till it seemed he'd drain the system dry. Other kids came in slow and went out quick, but Ritchie wasn't taking any notice of them: and he certainly didn't stop his groaning and swearing for the big figure looming vaguely behind him in the doorway.

"Strewth, Collins! You taking orders for those Hallowe'en masks?"

It was Des Banks on one of his routine checks.

Ritchie looked up, looked away, went on drying the blood on bits of lavatory paper.

"So who did this?" The deputy head was over and taking Ritchie's head in big, confident hands – using a handkerchief from his own breast pocket to dab at his lip. "Come on, Tiger, let's get you some first aid."

Ritchie went with the man. And when the first aid was

done – sitting in the secretary's room feeling like a right baby – Des Banks faced him, chair to chair, his long legs spread wide and his voice very reasonable.

"Well, Ritchie boy, you going to save my time by telling me?"

Ritchie looked at the floor. The man's voice went quite West Country when he was trying to be persuasive. Right back to his roots.

"I'm gonna find out. You could just give 6L their Economics lesson by saving time." He shook his head sadly. "And don't they need it!"

Ritchie shook his own. He wasn't going to say, and Des Banks knew he wasn't.

"Fair enough." The big man got up. "Don't go away, now."

He was gone about a quarter of an hour, while Ritchie cut off any conversation with the secretary by only grunting to her first question. It left him time to sit there wondering what Lucy would say when she saw him: because she'd be really upset. She'd probably know the truth of everything by now – they all would, from Sadie – and wouldn't she really feel sorry when she saw this lot?

Not that that was why he'd let it happen, of course.

The blood had stopped, the shaking was nearly over, and the sun was warming him through the office glass when Des Banks came back. "All right, Tiger, that's all done: and you don't even go in the witness box." He stood and stared his blue eyes at Ritchie. "You did well. Showed a bit of grit, by all accounts." He nodded, went on nodding before, "Pearson's parents are getting a final letter and the others will be dealing with me."

Ritchie got up. He wanted to be back in the classroom.

"But I thought it was Lucy Bowyer kept you awake at night." The big man smiled. "Anyhow, you'll live. Just stay away from mirrors for a year."

Ritchie caught up with his class in Maths. The lesson had already been disturbed by the inquisition, and from the way

47

everyone was sitting at their work without looking around, Ritchie guessed Mr Carew had already been driven to threatening them with capital punishment or something. Pearson wasn't there – he had Extra Something-else – but Pickett and Ryan were; and they were keeping their heads well down. No tight rein, though, could keep the rest from seeing Ritchie.

"Je-sus!" Sunil half got up.

"That's bad news!" said Tony. "Ritchie-boy..."

"All right, all right!" Mr Carew wasn't going to lose what he'd just fought for on a wave of sympathy for Collins. "Sit down, Collins, please, if you're feeling up to staying..."

And only now did Ritchie find out how hard it was to speak. It was as if his mouth was full of dentist's fingers. "Ye' shir..." He slid into a handy seat; saw Lucy staring, Sadie with her hands up to her face and crying. Mr Carew passed him a double sheet of paper torn from a book and a Bic from his pocket, pointed a finger at some questions on the blackboard.

It was shock, Ritchie decided, that was why Lucy hadn't smiled. It took people like that. Think of the school secretary when he'd walked in. Another split second of looking round and he'd have seen her wave a hand at him, or wink. But he wouldn't look round again now. Anyway, he couldn't, because the new girl was in that direction, too, and he didn't want to be forced into a wave to her which might be seen. Instead, he looked at the time on his scratched watch. They were coming up to the dinner break, and there'd be over an hour for things to happen. So he had a go at a couple of equations, and because they didn't matter they worked out nicely. Well, that was life, wasn't it? What he also resolved, though, was that he would stay put when the buzzer went: because it was only fair to give Lucy the chance to come to him. That was the least he could do. She'd want to make the move, seeing him hurt like this.

But, blast it, the first to come was Sadie. How stupid could he get, forgetting the reason for his beating up? In the immediate scrape of movement as Mr Carew walked out, she darted down the aisle, put an arm round his shoulder, and he was trapped. She brushed his face with her hair, wet with crying, and, "Those pigs!" she said. "I told Mr Banks what he said. Anyhow, I'm used to all that. But your *face...*" She hugged him fiercely, Ritchie managing a painful smile before she suddenly let go and went running out. Then Tony and Sunil took him with them, wanting details, threatening retaliation, sitting with him and watching him put his school dinner in his ear. But none of that counted: because what had him choked was what happened while Sadie was hugging him and the others were still coming over. Lucy walked on past; she must have, because one second he'd seen her coming through the threads of Sadie's hair, and the next the room was empty except for the three of them; Sunil holding the door and Tony hugging him like a brother; nothing like the way he wanted... What a killer!

He thought his mother would raise the Garrison Patrol when she saw his face. He had half an hour before she came in from answering Barry August's phone, and with clean clothes and flesh-tinted Clearasil he did his best to look less like Frankenstein's monster. But as she came in through the door she almost dropped the vodka bottle and new pyjamas she was carrying, crushed him to her, held him at arms' length, and, in the way people do, started blaming him for being a victim almost as fiercely as she swore at the yobs. It took a lot of painful talk and a start on the Smirnoff before Ritchie could persuade her not to go charging up to the school. "It's been...sorted," he said. "Des Banks...did ...well."

Immediately, she faced the next problem. "Dad's going to explode in that isolation ward. He's going to be so *frustrated.* When he sees you he's going to want to come out and kill that kid!" She put things away in the wrong places, crackled the pyjama wrapping as she hugged it and threw it down, went out to fill a kettle. "He's supposed to be kept

49

cheerful! They get depressed enough in isolation..."

To which there was only one answer, forced out slowly like everything Ritchie said, "I won't...come in. Wait... outside. Tell him I...got...cricket practice... You made me...not miss it..."

"Ritchie, you don't play cricket..."

"'S why I...need the...practice." They nodded at each other, a mute substitute for a laugh.

"I'll think of something, invent some tale. Come on, then, I'll get us a toasted sandwich while you try and make yourself look respectable."

Ritchie didn't attempt to answer that: just went all round again with spot cream.

At the hospital they were brought up short by the strictness of the new regime. The Ward Sister seemed a lot tougher than the M.O. Hardly looking up from her desk she reassured them that Sergeant Collins was as well as could be expected; and then she went briskly through the drill.

"You'll be the only ones," she said. "Normally it's only one chosen relative but we'll let your son in, too." She stared at Ritchie's face with an almost professional interest.

"Oh, he won't come in today, Sister. I don't want his father to see him looking like this."

But now the Sister actually smiled. She wasn't all that old, Ritchie decided, under that ridiculous head-dress military nurses have to wear. "You'll both be very well disguised. Hang your top coats up, please."

They put their summer tops on pegs and went round a corner from reception into a narrow corridor fitted up like the sink area of a small kitchen: but here the washing-up was of the surgical sort. Following the Sister's example they sprayed the soles of their shoes with antiseptic and washed their hands vigorously in a brown liquid-iodine soap, nudging off the taps with their elbows just like medics in all the films. From a plastic dispenser they pulled plastic aprons, and from another they pulled paper caps and masks.

"Now he won't know you from Adam!" the Sister said.

"Just keep your eyes out of trouble..."

This was all a novelty, and Ritchie felt strangely elated, doing the doctor bit. But if he got a secret lift from the dressing-up he was in for a real downer when they went in to see his father.

For a start, they didn't actually go in to see him. All their precautions were for the other patients who were coming out of their isolation, the Sister said, vulnerable people with reduced immunity who could be killed by a common cold – five young, bald and silent men preoccupied with Airfix models. Dick Collins was in a side room into which they could only stare through a small window, taking turns.

"We'll give him a fortnight of this. Intensive drugs. Then a week off, then another course..."

But Ritchie was hardly listening. His dad was asleep as if dead, his face as white as the pillow it was lying on, his hair fluffed up in a way he never combed it.

"He'll get nauseous and irritable. Sleep's a blessing."

"For a fortnight?"

"Of course not. He'll be up and about and walking round his room. He's got a fridge for soft drinks, his own bathroom off there, a television and a video machine. If he's got favourite videos, you bring them in. And special food – bring in what he likes. Tempt him, because he won't want to eat. We do it in the micro-oven: it sterilizes any germs..."

Ritchie and his mother were left in a stunned sort of silence. The thoroughness – and the pain – of the regime was very obvious now.

"You can talk to him two-way, on the phone over there..."

"Like prison visiting." June recovered with a little laugh. "So they tell me..."

What followed was a long, long silence in which Ritchie and his mother stared through the porthole, one after the other: and busy as she was, the Sister stayed.

"He'll be brighter tomorrow. I'll tell him you came..."

51

"Yes." But they didn't move. Ritchie wasn't going to be the first to walk away from his dad.

"Have they talked to you about donors, Mrs Collins?"

"Generally. I know the various options."

"Well, it's never too soon to start searching. Get it all lined-up if you can. That's one thing the patient can start feeling relaxed about."

"Sure." There was another long silence till June, with a little clucking noise in her throat, turned from the porthole and went from the ward, slowly, like someone walking away from a grave.

"Have you told...that Gran...over Essex?" Hard as it was to say anything through his swollen lips it seemed a straightforward enough question; but Ritchie knew it would catch his mother on the raw. He'd chosen a moment in the kitchen when her Lean Cuisine and his steak pie were about to come out of the oven, him busy getting the trays and making the coffee and her doing some salad for herself. There was a long tossing. His dad's relatives weren't really family at all: they were names hardly ever mentioned, no birthdays were remembered and Ritchie had never had a present from them in his life. All the family side of things came from his mother's people, and Ritchie's dad seemed quite happy about that. The earliest photographs only went back to the registry office wedding, and that seemed very one-sided. They didn't crop up in conversation, and the odd snappy answer had stopped Ritchie asking about them.

But now they *had* to be discussed, awkward or not. For a start they needed to be told his dad was so ill. But what was really important was contacting any brothers and sisters to see if one was a match. If his dad's best chance for a transplant was a brother or a sister then they had to be tested. Quick. And there were some sisters, that he did know. And hadn't he once heard his mum say 'brother', nastily, like in an argument?

In the kitchen, meanwhile, it was all oven gloves and foil

52

containers, plenty of business but no words – until they were balancing their trays in front of the News and she suddenly said, "I'll phone the old girl tonight. Had to wait till they were sure."

"What about...those...sisters? They're the ones. You got...their numbers?"

He knew she hadn't. The address book by the phone was an open affair, and there was only one other Collins in there, the gran in old ink: but suddenly he just felt the weird need to be putting a bit of pressure on.

June Collins shook her head; and the way she did it made it look as if she couldn't be expected to have their numbers, either. Ritchie forced himself not to react. Whenever a stray thought about the Collins family came, he always ended telling himself there was something mysterious in all this: *do not touch*, sort of thing. But now the time to touch had come. For a few seconds longer he sat watching as she put her unfinished tray on the floor and pushed it away with her foot, sank back in her chair and laid her hands along its arms like an Egyptian queen.

Now.

"Isn't there...some brother...I once...heard about as well?"

June didn't move; didn't blink; didn't even seem to breathe. "Really?"

"Yeah...I...think...so." He said it slowly, each word equally weighed.

She sighed now. Long, and from some very deep place. "Well, I'm not lying and saying there isn't." She stared at him: or was it through him. "But if there ever was I can tell you he hasn't been around for years and years..."

"Mum, get on that phone!" His own tray was down and he was up. "What are we waiting for? Can't we find out?"

But still she didn't move; just sat staring into space. And Ritchie's head went light. The pain of eating and talking had been forgotten. In facing his mother all he could see was his father, and not that deathly-looking stranger back there in the hospital bed, but the man in that special helmet, the real soldier, leading his men in their formation. *"He's my dad as well as your husband!"*

He thought she'd be angry, go for him. But she just closed her eyes, as if in pain. "Thank you, Ritchie," she said. "I needed that."

If she did ring anyone she went out of the flat to do it. Ritchie had a bath — saw where those bruises had spread and ripened — and heard the front door go a couple of times. Otherwise, she only answered a call from her mother in which she'd kept things very optimistic. But he knew he'd said enough. She'd get on to the Collins family tonight, or in the morning from the Barry August phone: because he knew she desperately wanted to sort things for his dad, every bit as much as he did. It was just there was this awkward something in the way of doing it.

Pearson wasn't at school the next day, and Ryan and Pickett had shifted their allegiance to a crowd of fifth-form drop-outs. But Ritchie wasn't bothered about the enemy; apart from his painful face, it was almost as if all that hadn't happened. And even Lucy Bowyer had had to fade slightly from the picture — temporarily, just while he sorted something life-and-death first: because this morning it was Sadie O'Connell he wanted to see; the new girl whose father knew all about *his* father and his illness. Today Ritchie needed to know the strength of the brother/sister thing in all this transplant business. How crucial were these people, and would one of them do, any one, or one of them especially? With these Collins' complications tangling around, Ritchie had to know how important the distant Essex family would have to be.

As soon as he spotted her, Ritchie could see that special army style at work: the fast fitting-in which showed she wouldn't be backward in making friends at this school, whether people like Pearson came to it or not. She was with a couple of girls in a recess by the library, sharing a magazine. Deliberately blind to anyone else, Ritchie hurried over and hovered near enough to let Sadie see him: and within the time it takes to close a book, she'd jumped up from the others and come over, seriously searching his face as if she were shining a torch around it.

"It's looking a bit better. Oh, Ritchie..." She put her hand on his shoulder.

"Don't worry about me – I'm a fast healer!" But he quickly needed her to know that this wasn't meant to be another gratitude time. "Listen, your dad – he's on my dad's ward, that's what you said...?"

"Not now; they've moved your dad for his treatment."

"Yeah, but he knows all the business, doesn't he; what goes on? All the transplant stuff?"

The slow way Sadie nodded told Ritchie she actually knew a fair bit about what was happening to his father. It was the sort of weighted nod you get in a quiz when you've got a clue right. "Well..." He coughed, put a hand to his mouth. This was the painful, difficult bit: but in the words themselves today, not in saying them. "Listen, do you reckon..."

But now Sadie was looking over Ritchie's shoulder; there was someone behind him; someone she wasn't sure whether she should smile at or not, like Des Banks, or...

Lucy. Ritchie angled an eye in a window to see the auburn hair; to see her hovering. His spirits lifted; but he'd just got to get this said, for his dad. He turned his head and tried to smile at her; but with his swollen mouth he couldn't be sure how it came out.

Like yesterday she was just looking.

"Listen, could I come round and see him, your dad, have a word with him...about mine?"

Sadie's eyes came back to him; and he knew that Lucy had drifted away.

"Yeah, if you like. Come after school, he's on early today..."

"Ta."

Ritchie stayed just long enough for politeness before he

moved away to look for Lucy. But she'd gone – and gone quickly. And with Games and various options, that was the way she was all day – inaccessible to Ritchie, who was left to take a sort of martyr's refuge in poor work and gloomy thoughts about his dad.

He was really impressed with Sadie's father. The man was no taller than Ritchie, looked him easily in the eye, was quietly spoken with a warm smile and a way about him which didn't try to blind you with science. At the same time he didn't treat you like an idiot, either. Her mother wasn't in – she was an agency nurse out on call – but somehow Ritchie guessed she'd have sat round with them and shown the same interest as the others: it seemed to be that sort of friendly family. Like the hospital sister, Mr O'Connell gave a quick professional eye to Ritchie's face, and with a firm hand on his shoulder he talked about how racism was a greater danger than anything else the country needed to arm itself against. And then, after congratulating Ritchie – not thanking him – for the stand he'd made, they went on to talk about his dad.

"What they told your mother, that's true enough," Mr O'Connell said. "There's always got to be a one in four chance of a brother or sister coming up with the same bone marrow type. It's like this" – he stroked his small moustache with his fingers before holding them up as if conducting a miniature orchestra – "each one's always one in four; but the odds go up the more there are – twenty-five per cent, forty-four per cent, fifty-eight per cent – it's all very mathematical..."

Ritchie nodded, but with a frown. "What I don't get is where do they get the four from in the first place. It's always one or two or three in *four*..."

"Well now, look, everyone's got a mother an' a father, haven't they? Hang on a jiffy..." He went out to a removal crate in the passage and came back with a notebook and a ball pen. "See here, there's a mother and a father, and their

56

children take half their own genes from each one of them..." He wrote 'F' and 'M' at the top of a page under the spiral. "Now, the father's the same as everyone else – he's made up of two sets of genes himself, all right? – one from each of *his* parents, so we'll give him 'a' for his father and 'b' for his mother..." He wrote the letters beneath the 'F'. "And the mother's made up of two sets as well, so we'll give her 'c' for her father's genes and 'd' for her mother's." He started to draw little mapping lines between the parents' gene halves. "Now then, one child will turn out 'ac', another will turn out 'bc', and one will be 'ad' and another 'bd'. Possibly. If they're all different. But then they could all be the same, 'ac' if you like; but the chance of two brothers or sisters coming up the same is always going to be one in four because there's only four permutations before everything starts repeating..."

He smiled, sat back, turned the paper round for Ritchie to get a clearer look: and now Ritchie began to see. If Dick Collins' dad's genes were called 'a' and 'b' and his mother's, the Essex gran's, were called 'c' and 'd', then Dick Collins was one letter from each – and so were the two sisters and the possible brother, with that one in four chance of any of them being the same.

"Being his son, Ritchie, you can only be a half-match to your dad at the best, because your mother's genes are in you, too..."

"Yeah, I see..." Ritchie nodded slowly; it was a complicated thing to grasp.

"We're not talking about blood groups, be sure about that now, won't you? This is tissue type of the little cells made in the marrow of your bones. And if they don't match up when you do a transplant, the body rejects them; and that's a battle we never win..." He stroked his moustache again, a finger each side, and stared seriously at Ritchie as if making it right for being too blunt with him.

"Anyhow, Ritchie's dad's got two," Sadie put in. "That right, Ritchie? Two definite sisters and the chance of a brother..."

"So they reckon." It's amazing how much gets said in a polite walk home with someone.

Mr O'Connell spread his hands. "So there's fifty-eight per cent chance of one of them being right. Not too bad, eh? Could be worse. The thing to do is get them in quickly and get them tissue-typed – it's painless, you know. Then you can start working out your alternatives..."

For the past thirty-six hours Ritchie had wanted to sit by a phone with the Essex gran's number and a pad for writing down her daughters'. Now all he wanted to do was get out of Sadie's house as quickly as possible and stand over his mother till she'd done it. But there was one more question he wanted answered while he was there.

"They told my mum there were other ways, too. Like, his own bone marrow put back, and strangers who match..."

Mr O'Connell nodded. "That's right. Your best chance is always a matched relative, though."

"But why just the one chance? Why not..."

"Why not try all three, you're asking?" Mr O'Connell shut his notebook and placed it on to the table by his chair. While he thought, he carefully lined up the ball pen next to it; wasn't satisfied, lined it up another way, then picked pad and pen up again. "The reason why is before we transplant we irradiate the patient's body, we kill the cells. It's what fall-out does and nuclear leaks do. Radioactivity. We do it so we can start all over again..."

Ritchie swallowed, gave the smallest of nods.

"But the body usually only takes one go at that. I've never known it done more than once."

His mouth had gone dry. It was a very quiet, straight moment, with Sadie sitting there not moving, and her father back at his moustache.

"Yes, we have just the one crack at it. An' that's why it's got to be the best chance going."

"Yeah... I get that."

Mr O'Connell stood up. He'd been kind and helpful, but there were clearly other things to do in the new quarters. "So, if you can find your dad's siblings get onto it quick – because if there isn't a match, we'll need to try to find someone unrelated off the register."

Ritchie got up, too. "And what's the –" he weighed his palms like balances – "like, the chances?"

The man looked at him. "Now boy, sensible medics don't talk in chances and all that palaver – chances are for bookmakers and newspaper reporters. Certainly go for your matched sibling first, but I tell you, wherever there's a chance at all it's well worth taking. And we get some very good results off the Anthony Nolan Register..."

But Ritchie felt too close to a real answer to let anyone get off the hook. He wouldn't move; almost felt ungrateful at not buying the soft soap. But a finger went to his own fluffy, puffy moustache as if to remind the man of a slight favour. "Come on," he said quietly. "Please tell me."

"But I can't, boy!" The man very nearly walked out of the room: but he didn't, he stared Ritchie square in the eye with a look which said this was special. "All right, then, for what it's worth – and things change daily in this field, remember – you can put your non-relative match at something less than fifty-fifty. Less than half a chance. Re-using the patient's own bone marrow, it's too new to say. But a matched sibling, now, for a man about your father's age and otherwise fit an' well – top whack, an eighty per cent chance, I'd say..."

"Eighty..."

"His age is on his side, and his fitness. But don't you go quoting me, now, or I'll be back to Aldershot..."

"No. Course not. Yeah, well...thanks very much." Suddenly Ritchie's inside felt the way his face looked, all beaten up. Put in percentages even eighty was a fair way short of a hundred. But it was better than fifty, wasn't it?

"We do fight like hell for every one..."

"Yes, I know. Thanks very much, Mr O'Connell..."

59

Sadie went with him to the door. He'd forgotten the new girl in the eye to eye.

"Thanks for that," Ritchie said, somehow not managing to call her by her name. "Yeah, thanks a lot."

"That's all right."

Quickly, he ran off, his mind filled with percentages and this weird word, siblings. Two siblings, possibly three; fifty-eight per cent of an eighty per cent chance. Top whack. So what did that work out at? When it mattered his Maths always deserted him. But to his great delight he ran home to the news that June had rung the Essex Collinses. "I'm going to see his mother tomorrow. At two o'clock."

"I'm coming, then."

"You are not!" And something in her eye told him that he most certainly wasn't, either. "You're going to school."

"Why not? Why can't I come?"

"Oh, lovely – your face is a bit better. You only look ugly now. Change your shirt, Ritchie, and we'll get up to the hospital."

"Why can't I come?"

*"Change your shirt, Ritchie!"*

And he knew for sure that whatever family mystery there was, he wasn't going to find out just like that. Because it was serious. It was definitely serious. But at least she was going, the ball was rolling, and that was the main thing, wasn't it?

So he changed his shirt and went to see his dad, disguised again behind his mask. And his dad was sitting up, washed-out but pleased to see them, and waving with what Ritchie suddenly decided was about eighty per cent of a normal smile.

# CHAPTER FOUR

There'd be something about the way June Collins turned
the corner and parked her car which would tell Ritchie all
about how she'd got on. From the living room he had a
clear view of the run-in to the flats and the islands of oil
patches which marked the parking places. He'd watched out
for her at all sorts of different times, when all there was in it
was pocket money or having someone in. And he reckoned
he knew: how, in a good mood, she came in carefully and
parked well to one side in her usual space: but when Barry
August's customers had given her a bad time, she revved up
to the *No Parking* bay near the steps and left her car
without locking it. She only cared about things like that
when she wanted to.

Ritchie had thought she might be back before him, but he
had to wait quite a while, imagining Blackwall Tunnel delays at the best, or some terrible family row at the worst. So
he could only watch, still charged up with what Mr O'Connell had said, keeping himself ready for anything. When she
came, though – and there was never any mistaking the roar
of her engine – he was relieved to see her drive in slowly and
park over in her own spot. Everything was all right, then.
They hadn't given her a bad time. He uncrossed his fingers
and ran to reboil the kettle; switched the television on and
sat down. And missed hearing the car door slam hard
enough to set the vehicle rocking.

She'd gone to town on her appearance all right. Looking
more as if she'd been up for an award than out on a
life-and-death mission, she'd certainly given them the works
over in Essex: new hair, sexy suit, all the matching bits and
pieces, and an actressy smile to go with it. As he saw her

come in through the door he half expected to be called 'Ritchie-darling'.

"Shit!" she said. "Broke a nail in the Tunnel, changing gear behind a stupid bus..." But she was watching his eyes: they both knew they weren't into *have-you-had-a-good-day?* and all that nonsense: this was some sort of verdict time. She dropped her car keys into the fruit bowl and started riffling through the letters on the sideboard, all the usual delays before the bad news.

"They'll do it," she said, addressing the top of Ritchie's head. "We phoned both his sisters while I was there. One came round – May, she lives near – and I had a long talk with Eileen on the phone. Really upset at the news but they're both ringing the hospital to make appointments. Tomorrow. And more than prepared to be tested and be the donor, if it's one of them..." She threw open her arms like a magician's assistant, one foot thrust forward.

"Great!" Ritchie jumped up, would have hugged his mother, except her smile was as stagey as her pose: the sort you suddenly see the wrinkles in. "They're not hanging about, then, are they? An' has he got a brother? Did you get to him?"

He could have been lobbing a grenade. Out of nowhere June suddenly threw down the letters in her hand and shouted at him, flipped – just like that, no warning.

"No, I didn't!" she shrieked. "It hasn't exactly been bloody easy today. My God!" She waved a braceleted hand at his face. "Getting beaten up's a doddle, I tell you, compared with what I've had!" She swung on her heel and ran from the room with a slam, all before he'd drawn his next breath.

"Christ Almighty!" He picked up the letters off the floor, put them back on the mantelpiece. *What string got pulled there?* In the kitchen the kettle boiled and clicked off; while Ritchie went back to the window to check where the car was. He'd thought he knew his mother. But this was a new complication, which he definitely didn't understand.

62

Like just about everyone with a close relative in hospital, it hadn't taken long for Ritchie to discover how hospital visiting could hit the heights of drama and dive to some pretty boring lows. And that held true even when the visiting was through a small window and all the talking was on a telephone. There's no smaller small-talk in the world than the drama of what next door's cat did, and no words to hang on to with a tighter grip than *What did the doctor say?* Some bowel movements you'd report in bold headlines; some deaths you wouldn't wrap the chips in. Some half hours were a day, others were thirty seconds.

But the following night's visit was a big one: when the M.O. would have been round with his team to tell Dick Collins how successful the treatment was proving. There might also be news, Ritchie hoped, of when his dad's sisters were going in for their tests.

Being patient and thorough with the scrubbing up was difficult, and Ritchie and June both tried to get into the same overall: but their eyes lit up in turns as they peered through the window to see Dick Collins actually sitting up, looking as if he'd been waiting for them. On his locker-top was a wicker basket in its early stages next to a cheap book of crosswords; his hair had been combed his own way and he had his wrist watch on.

"You're looking pleased with yourself!" June told him down the phone. "Which nurse have you got under that bed?"

Dick smiled, the old no-answer to her outrageousness. He hunched his shoulders, showed her an innocent pair of hands.

"You look miles better. M.O. been round?"

Ritchie wondered if her nervousness got lost through the intercom, or amplified. But Dick gave an army thumbs up.

"O.K.! On course. Responding."

"Is that what he said?"

"That's what he said to me."

"Good! That's great! How do you feel?"

"Oh, not so dusty." He pulled a face, touched the top of his head. "Got that Kojak feeling coming on!" He waved behind her at Ritchie.

"You were going bald anyway, my lad!"

"How are things, Ritch?" He really was making an effort.

"O.K. Yeah. Great. Got most of my Maths right." And like an idiot Ritchie almost told him his mouth was nearly better. Instead, he came to the point. "Have they told you your sisters are coming in for tests?"

Dick nodded, no smile now. "May and Eileen. That's good news, eh?"

"Say when, did they?"

"Tomorrow, Hitler said."

"That's quick. Then how long before they know?" The question had followed on naturally. It was out of Ritchie's mouth before he realised the huge importance hanging on such casual words.

"Soon. They take it over to Tooting. Just a motor-cycle ride each way."

"Good. That's good, eh?"

"Yeah, very good. Hope so."

And that was almost it: except that there was one more question Ritchie was daring himself to ask, and now seemed to be the time to pluck up the guts to ask it. Or was it? Ritchie chickened for a bit. "So it's all going all right? The man said?"

"He did." Dick signalled Ritchie to wait, put down his phone and unbuttoned his pyjama jacket. On his shaved chest a small tube protected in plaster stuck out, and on the back of his hand another sealed-off line lay taped. He made exaggerated pointing gestures at them. "They feed the drug through this, saves a lot of injections; and they take a blood sample every day from the hand." He pulled a confident face, nodded. "And the blood count's moving back to normal: no kidology, I've seen the graphs."

Ritchie gave a thumbs up back, heard his mother cough,

knew she wanted to get in on the congratulations. But not for a minute. That other question still sat raw on Ritchie's lips: and now he had to ask it.

"Isn't there another one to try as well? For testing? Did I dream you've got a brother, too?"

It was out, and God, it had hurt. He could see it in the eyes. His father's mood changed as suddenly as when a car runs up a safe pavement. The man stared at him in some sort of shock, then he frowned, that old frown of disapproval.

"What gave you that stupid idea?"

"I thought . . ."

"You thought wrong. I haven't got a brother. June! What the hell's been going on?" Now he sounded in real pain.

"Nothing! He's heard nothing from me!" Ritchie and June found themselves tussling for a hold of the telephone.

"Let's have that straight, Ritchie!"

"All right!" Ritchie blew into his mask. Yes, his dad was getting better – better enough to be hated for the minute. *"All right!"* he said. "Sorry." But he hadn't got the mouthpiece any more.

"Dick, I don't know what he's on about. Listen, Army Welfare rang today, they're sorting out your National Insurance stuff. And the chaplain called. Sent you his best wishes." She croaked a laugh as false as anything Ritchie had ever heard in his life. "Bet he'd turned the town over to find you a get-well card with motorbikes on it!"

But Dick Collins wasn't laughing. And Ritchie knew the look; he was well used to it. When things upset him, when an order wasn't obeyed or something didn't get done properly, he stayed upset for ages. He couldn't throw off a bad mood – or pretend to – the way June could. And right now, true to form, he was leaving her to do the talking, just sitting there, hardly bothering to nod. Ritchie stayed just in view so as not to make things worse by going off and sulking. But he was looking carefully at the pair of them.

So whose fault was it that he'd ruined tonight's visiting? Was it his fault that he'd tried to sort out something vital?

How was it down to him if his dad couldn't own up to having a brother for some reason – because he *had* heard talk of a brother sometime in the past. He hadn't dreamt it, he was certain. No! His belly fluttered with a sudden anger. He'd only stepped into the mess. He hadn't made it!

"Come on, say good-bye to your dad, Ritchie." His mother handed him the telephone – muttering in his ear: "Then we'll go and pick up your Peace prize!"

When Lucy Bowyer asked after his dad the next day, Ritchie really had to check that he wasn't still back at home in his bed. He'd often had experiences the other way – lie-in dreams where he'd got up and gone to the bathroom only to find he hadn't moved; and his first stupid thought was that this was the same sort of thing, just the other way around.

So it was an awkward meeting, because quite apart from their rift, meeting a dream image takes a lot of facing out!

"Ritchie..."

"Oh. Hello." He wanted to make it easy but he didn't know how. He knew he mustn't assume they were back to what they'd been before, but then he didn't want to seem too off-hand.

"Er, how's your dad getting on, now?" She was standing off-balance, awkward for a change. He saw she wasn't smiling: but then her mouth wasn't all tight with dislike either.

"All right." He nodded, looked hopeful. It didn't seem to be the time to go into details. "How's yours?"

"All right."

And now the long silence that comes before the real business. Kids they hardly saw went past them through the gates into the school. A car screeched somewhere and neither looked round. Perhaps Lucy might use her line about Tracy Brown, or he might start on about power station chimneys. Something desperately needed saying, that was for sure: but neither said it. No-one likes making false moves, reading things wrong and leaving themselves looking stupid. And Ritchie was definitely one of those who'd sooner go home and regret it than take the chance of an insult.

"That's good news," he managed, getting no further forward. So they stood there trying to read each other's faces like infants with new books, a good metre apart. Sadie would have touched. Pearson would have pushed. But Ritchie and Lucy just stood there staring.

"Well, my dad says get well soon," she came out with at last – and with a sudden swing of her auburn hair she went running into school.

Later, of course, when the moment had long passed, he went over and over how he'd blown it, how timid he'd been. What was up with him, he asked himself in History (Oliver Cromwell) and in Science (Leonardo da Vinci) that he couldn't go more boldly for what he wanted? Why was it only in dreams when he was the man? Because in Mathematics (a little logic) he realised that Lucy hadn't needed to say anything if she'd wanted to stay at arm's length. And even if he'd taken a chance and been slapped down, well, was that the end of the world right now? She'd done her bit and he hadn't been able to find the easy words. But the worst of it was, and he slammed the thought into his tin locker after P.E., she definitely wouldn't come up with an opening like that again.

In that miserable mood of what-might-have-been Ritchie dragged on home after school, back to another couple of hours in the fridge with his mother. And somehow, the way things seemed to be going, he wasn't thrown nearly as badly as he might have been by the rotten news she had for him.

They'd phoned it through from the hospital only minutes before; she was still pacing up and down, jacket in her hand, when Ritchie walked in.

"They're no good," she said, flatly. "Eileen and May. They tested them this morning, and they don't match. They're no good as donors." She swore in a new way. "It's just come through."

Ritchie swallowed and looked at her: and all at once she

wasn't so much his mother any more as just another worried and frightened human being. Perhaps it was the language she'd used. Or was there a moment when a family thing like theirs – mother and son – changes? When the problem you face reduces you to just being two *people*. At any rate, that moment, for the first time in his life, he saw June Collins as a person and not as his mother. For him, the news had come too suddenly to be properly understood at first; he hadn't been getting ready to think about the results of the tests because he'd not expected them so soon. Now he just stood there shaking his head.

"Oh, Christ! *Oh, Christ!*" He slung his plastic bag into a chair. This hadn't been part of what was to happen. In his mind, once the brother had been written off, one of the sisters *had* to be o.k. His dad was supposed to be one of the eighty per cent of successes, so Ritchie wasn't settling for anything less.

He sat down. "Well," the new equality between them came out as an edge to his voice, "I s'pose we're just gonna have to find that brother he hasn't got!" He stared at her, waited for her to get angry again.

She stared back, minute movements of her pupils darting between his own eyes, weighing-up, understanding – until with a violent shake of her head she disagreed. "He won't have it, Ritchie, do what you like. Just don't start disturbing the ground. May and Eileen didn't work, there's no reason why a third one will." She scrabbled in her handbag and pulled out a twisted pamphlet. *The Truth About Transplants.* She waved it at him. "Look! It's been in all the papers. The Register of Donors. There are thousands, and they're very successful..."

Ritchie kept his voice deliberately low; but it was throaty and getting angry. "Do you know the different chances? Well, I've found out, and the chances are thirty per cent better with a brother..."

"Where'd you get that?" Still she waved the pamphlet. "The one thing they never do is talk percentages. The samples are too small. You're dreaming that up. All I know is what they say in here, and this is it as far as I'm concerned." She was waving the paper more violently, getting angry herself.

But only to match Ritchie. "What's up with you? You're worse than kids, you two! Doesn't someone's life count more than some old quarrel?"

"Shut up!" June Collins shrieked. She shook every hair of her head at him in her fury. "Don't you think I care as well? His brother's gone – for good!" At last she got rid of her jacket, threw it down on the floor as if she'd send it through the carpet. She twisted herself away and slammed through into the kitchen. "Don't you come it with me, Ritchie!" She was fighting to get hold of her voice. "And if you're in that mood you'd better not come to the hospital either. Your dad's going to be down enough, thank you *very much*!" Suddenly she came back, an angry face through the door. "There's one real chance, and that's what we're taking. We're going for the Register, tomorrow. And don't you ever forget, Ritchie Collins, I want your dad well every last bit as much as you do!"

In a draught of door she went out again and threw together a noisy tea: while Ritchie took himself off to his room, pitched himself onto his bed and lay there shutting his mind to what she'd just said. Not her wanting his dad to get well bit, there was never any doubt about that: but how could anyone settle for second best when there was still a chance of something better? No, he just wasn't going to accept what they were saying, his mother and his father. If the brother was alive it had to be possible to find him, wherever he was in the world. Good God, they even did television programmes about this sort of thing, didn't they?

But what to do to change his parents' minds, that was the problem? The least they could do was have a good try – but how to make them? Ritchie suddenly sat up. All right, then – what if it was down to him to find this brother? He could have a go, couldn't he? He bent over and thumped his pillow. He didn't care what they said, he was going to give his dad a crack at the best chance going. And he immediately slumped back again, a Coke without the fizz. Because *what?* Without their help what could he do? Especially with time the way it was – running out fast...

He got no homework done. Homework right then was the least of all his worries: he was trying to find the answer to a question a lot more important than something off a practice paper. With his mother gone off to the hospital – on her own, as she threatened – he suddenly locked up the flat and headed for the medics' quarters. For reassurance: for the reassurance he needed from the new girl's father that it was definitely worth the search before he went out on such a thin limb: that what he'd been told was full strength, and, if it was, that he was *right* to be pushing for this mystery brother. And what all that amounted to in his mind was a bit of backing.

What he came away with, though, was a lot more than that. In the end it was real hope and determination that ran his feet home for him, and all down to Sadie O'Connell, too. But that was later.

When he arrived, her father told him how sorry he was the two sisters hadn't worked out: and he took great care to caution Ritchie that there was no better hope of a brother matching. But he also made it crystal clear that while the success rate with outside donors was a good one, a sibling who matched would be the best chance for Ritchie's father, without any doubt.

Ritchie, still upset and tense, listened to him carefully: and only when he'd heard him out, had the backing he needed, could he sit and relax just a bit and be something like himself again.

Which is where Sadie did her best to help. As if sensing how strung-up he was, she had quickly changed into an out-of-school sleeveless top which showed her shoulders and come to sit relaxed with her feet tucked up in a chair. Now,

70

when Ritchie had got everything straight again, she took him into the kitchen for a Coke.

She let him get that first half-glassful down; still painful; then in a quiet voice, more to the formica surface, she asked, "What do you reckon's up with your uncle, Ritchie? Why can't they find him?" She plopped more ice into his glass, brought back the life.

And just as quietly he told her: about the way no-one ever talked about his father's family, and what both his parents had said about the brother. He found himself telling her about the anger and the awkwardness, and, on a second Coke, about something he'd never really put into words before, not even to himself. About how bad he'd always felt that half his family background had been so cut off from him.

And it was easy saying it because Sadie was nodding, was with him. He was talking to a fellow sufferer. "You're not the only one, Ritchie." Her Oriental eyes opened wide when she was emphatic. "I don't go round telling people either, but when my mum came across the border into Hong Kong with the students, it was one really stormy night when the guards didn't think anyone would dare to make a run for it. But *her* mum and dad were supposed to come, too: only they didn't make it, the storm went away too quickly and the moon shone. So they had to stay behind; and mum hasn't heard a single word from them since." The girl looked down into her glass. "She wanted to go back, but they wouldn't let her." Ritchie followed the formica pattern with his eyes. The fridge chattered. "So that's my mum's family *I* haven't got..."

"Yeah." Ritchie looked at her: it was unbelievable the stories people sat on; the dramas.

Now Sadie was bending over him, hands flat on the table, shoulders up. "But I tell you what. *I'd* have gone back across that border." Her face was deadly serious. "And you can cross the river to see if this uncle's real, can't you? When's half-term?"

"Week after next." Suddenly he was ashamed and smiling

71

and excited all at once.

"And your dad's got another full treatment to go, so you've got a bit of time ..."

"I s'pose so." He'd take her word for that: her family were the experts.

"Then we can look up some maps tomorrow — and go on a scout the day after: that's Saturday..." Now he *was* sitting up. Her enthusiasm took him by surprise. "... Yeah? I'll come, Ritchie. Be company, the first time. Bit of help. Eh?" She'd drawn a chair up, was a conspirator at the same table already.

"Yeah, I don't mind. Why not?" Without thinking, his hand went to a shiny shoulder, patted it. "Thanks, Sayd..." And, quite surprised by the buoyancy he felt, Ritchie said his goodbyes and hurried to be home before his mother; because he had a plan now, a secret plan, and he wanted to keep it like that.

He ran hard all the way, but tonight for some reason he didn't seem to get short of breath: perhaps because the more serious thought in his head was that he was actually going to do something for his dad. It was a strong mix of emotions — this being the best chance, with him geared up to having a go at bringing it off: and a confused feeling of thanks to this new friend, which was different, somehow, to the way he'd be feeling about Tony or Sunil or Gerry.

And Sadie remembered to take in a map with her the next day: with her violin, her music case and her homework — nothing forgotten. Ritchie had wanted to, but just when he'd thought his mother was locked in the bathroom, he'd nearly been caught at the address book. In his panic, he'd been pleased just to get out with the Essex gran's address. On top of which the flat had been too quiet since the upset and there just hadn't been a right moment to go rummaging around for road maps. He had to tread very carefully if he was going to pull this off. He was going to need the secrecy and the skill of a good spy.

He'd twisted in bed half the night working out his excuses for getting away – on the Saturday and probably some of the days of half term – and then all that had suddenly and very neatly fallen into place. Lying there and burping on all the Coke he'd drunk, he remembered the lift his spirits had had when it had been poured; the enthusiasm in Sadie O'Connell, her pretty, eager face as she'd egged him on. And he was delighted with the thought. Sadie O'Connell! She could be his cover. He knew that someone like his mother wouldn't object to a bit of romance. He could make out he was soft on her and they were having a few days out while the weather was good. Judging by the sad business over Lucy Bowyer, old June wouldn't frown at a bit of sweet dreams – she'd even rinse him a shirt and make sure he had some fare money! Now Sadie remembering a map the next day was just a sign of how right he'd been...

Looking like a couple of conspirators – too casual for words – they took it into the library at dinner–time; a yellow AA book of a few years before. "Least it'll give us an idea," Sadie told him. "Then we can go for the rail or bus maps in the rack."

She was different today, Ritchie thought: like she'd been before in school; but in between he'd seen her at home, when she hadn't been the new girl at all, more grown-up and in charge. Now she was a new mix of the two.

"Don't you reckon?"

"Yeah. It's Hornchurch Elms we're looking for."

"Hornchurch Elms..." Quickly she had her finger in the Greater London page. "Be near Hornchurch, then. I've heard of that." Together they searched the fine squares on the right-hand side of the double opening and eventually they found it, faintly marked like a small town or a village.

"It's on this road just off the A13," he said, "nearest big place looks like Rainham. I'll get the bus map."

But that wasn't so easy. Mrs Craddock sat on her library as if all the books were her eggs. She'd go along the shelves turning them occasionally – and she reluctantly had to let

73

some go — but she was always very pleased when they were back under her wing. And that even went for London Transport give-away bus maps.

"That's a reference copy," she told Ritchie as he picked it up. "You're not to take it away."

"No, Mrs Craddock. I'm only over there."

She nodded and watched it go, off into an outer zone.

Homing in on Rainham, Ritchie quickly found Hornchurch Elms; then he traced a light green number all the way back along Ripple Road and Newham Way to the Blackwell Tunnel.

"723," he said. "Green Line. That's easy, then. One bus through the Blackwall Tunnel and the Green Line all the rest of the way."

But Sadie seemed to be there already. "We can find where they live and give it a look. It's easier to plan what to do when you can see something for real..." The words fell out fast and enthusiastic.

"Right." On the third go he got the map folding back inwards, ready to return.

"What's the address?"

"Twelve, The Street. Sounds small all right." He had a quick and ungrateful thought. If the place was that small and out in the country, a Chinese-looking girl wasn't exactly going to get lost in the background. But already the ball was rolling, and it wouldn't be stopped.

"What time tomorrow, then? No, tell you what, my set's got Library this afternoon. I'll stay now and look up the timetables, eh?"

"Cheers. Thanks, Sadie." Anyway, whether she was going to stand out or not, it was good having someone to share this with. Even old Sunil wouldn't have been this much help.

"O.K." She suddenly shut the map and turned to look him straight in the eye. "And wasn't I 'Sayd' last night?"

"Yeah..." Why was there always something awkward in people's names? Some trap? Ritchie's healing lip started hurting with a small rush of blood to the face. It had been a choice he'd known he was making. "I wasn't sure what you like being called."

Sadie didn't bat an eye. "Anything friendly," she told him. "It's not the name, is it, more how it's said. Only what you said just then sounded all businesslike..."

Ritchie laughed, looked round the library, dropped his voice to say, "Sorry!"

"No-one else calls me 'Sayd'..."

Ritchie nodded. Had he missed his gear somehow? He wasn't sure he wanted to be that special. But she *was* being very helpful. "I'll see you later, then, Sayd," he said: and it came out all wrong, not a bit like the night before. He scooped up the bus map, put it back in its place and hurried to his first afternoon class.

He spent the first part of the afternoon on measuring the face drawing of an airpump, ready to turn it through a plane to the cross-section. Craft Design Technology he enjoyed, especially when it was tricky and he had to concentrate; the trouble was, there was so much buzzing through his mind today he had a sort of nostalgia for this same piece of work as it had been last week when he'd peacefully started on it. A lot had happened since he'd slid this away in the folder. He rested his set square and capped his Rotring pen. There was the Lucy business, the illness, the quarrel. He'd never ever been at odds with his mum and dad before, not like this, not to the point where he was planning to lie and deceive. He stared around the room, saw movement in the corridor outside, caught Des Banks' eyes as he looked over the frosted glass of the door the way he always did. And the man winked: like a conspirator, too, off on some trail. Well, there you went. Do something new and you started seeing it done everywhere...

He turned back to his drawing: but before he knew it the buzzer was sounding, and already it was all change. God, where had that forty minutes gone? And he was still waving his work dry as the rest of his tutor group came in from their set options, started throwing bags onto seats to save

75

them for after break. And that included Lucy. Ritchie's paper waving stopped and she, instead of hurrying out again to the yard, quietly edged her way round the tables – to come and sit in the seat in front of him.

She faced him, smiled, put her hand on his work to lower it. "Ritch, I'm sorry about...you know...all that stuff. Made a right mess of everything. Didn't reckon for a minute...like, what was up with your dad..."

Ritchie just wanted to hug her. Straight from one of his dreams, this was! Everything coming out all right; the old walking-into-the-sunset touch. He was shocked and elated both at once, and he couldn't even put his mouth round a quick smile.

"Cheers...Luce," he said. And his inside crashed over as he nearly called her *Sayd*. "Me, too; I was..."

Lucy leaned closer. "Tomorrow, eh? Kiss and make up?"

"I don't mind." Now he smiled – and just as suddenly wanted to bash his face onto the top of the desk: and not in any frenzy of joy. How unfair could things get? "Only, not tomorrow. I've got something on for my dad. You know... But Sunday. I'm all right for Sunday..." His voice was bright and excited, the fluttering ribbon on a surprise knot of guilt which had him tight: a guilt he definitely didn't deserve. He rattled on about Greenwich Park, going back to count the chimneys, some stupid talk.

"O.K. Sunday. I'll just have to be patient, if it's for your dad..."

"Yeah. It is... It's important, like." Which it was: but his voice had gone very thin as if he were lying; he could hear it. Why couldn't he tell her about what he was doing with Sadie? He would if it was Sunil. It wasn't as if he *liked* Sadie like that, was it? But while Lucy squeezed his hand – his clammy hand – he knew he was lying to her; lying by omission. Lucy got up, went over to throw her bag on a chair well away from him.

Still, sometimes a little white lie works best...

But not when all the winds of fate are blowing against

76

you. Inner city winds, filled with all the garbage. Not when Sadie O'Connell just happens to poke her head round the tutor room door.

"Sorry, I'm in a rush, Ritch, late for violin. They're every hour from the Blackwall Tunnel, Saturdays. Nine o'clock, my place, all right? See you..." And she went.

While all Ritchie could do was sit there and nod. And swear. And listen to the door banging twice: once for Sadie in a rush; once for Lucy. And hear what she had shouted, "Forget it!"

Who ever said there was any natural justice in this life? he asked himself. *Him*, Ritchie Collins, looking like a liar and a cheat! Just when things seemed to be coming right. What chance was there for straight blokes in a world which treated them like this?

# CHAPTER FIVE

Of course, it rained. In your imagination, in advance, summer events hardly ever get rained on; the sun shines and the pictures in the head are as well-lit as film. But let the day be important enough in real life, and down comes the rain. It had happened at so many displays that Ritchie wasn't at all surprised when he woke to the wet on his window. It wasn't a deterrent: but it did make his plans with Sadie hard to justify to June.

"You're not still going in this!" she said. "You'll get soaked just waiting for a bus."

Ritchie looked out again. It wasn't just raining now, it was tipping it down. "It's not much. We'll be all right."

"You're very keen, Ritchie Collins." She looked at him hard.

"I'm just showing her London. She don't know it very well."

"Doesn't."

It did sound weak, he knew; really off-beam for him. Even on a nice day, the idea of him prowling round London like a tourist would have been very far-fetched.

"So will you be back to see your dad this afternoon?"

Ritchie walked out of the kitchen. She knew damned well he wouldn't, he'd explained that the night before. Now he suddenly didn't care whether he pleased her with what he was doing or not. This secret service stuff wasn't for *him*, was it? It was all for his dad. "I told you about that," he shouted to her. "I've done him a card and made him a tape off his Beatles album. I said I'll see him tomorrow."

The decision in his voice seemed to shut her up. He checked his watch, military style with a big arm movement.

78

Anyway, it was time to make a move. He just hoped Sadie wasn't having any hassle getting out in this. They'd arranged to meet at Safeways which was a heck of a wet walk away if she wasn't coming. But that was a chance he'd have to take...

She was there. Along the way – running thoughts – he imagined how he'd be feeling if it was a day out with Lucy. Greenwich Park with his feet not quite touching the ground, the sun suddenly shining, the long grass. And even on a mission like today's, wouldn't it be great, just being together again, a pair? She'd be a bit late and then knock him for six with something she was wearing or the way she'd done her hair. And she'd say something which'd catch him right down in the pit of his stomach.

Some hope any more!

And it was Sadie who was there, wrapped up in a hooded raintop and looking as damp as the day. She smiled. It was great she was helping, but he wanted to groan with the unfairness of it all; with the demolition job she'd done on him and Lucy.

"Cheers for coming, Sayd."

"Lovely day, isn't it?"

Already they were in the way, standing between the Saturday shoppers and the trolleys they were grabbing, so they ran for a shop doorway by the 108 bus stop. Ritchie wiped his face with a hankie, tried to think of something to say. Sadie pulled back her hood and shook her hair, lifted it from underneath with her fingers: somehow a private thing to do, as if she were a sister or something. "I won't tell you where this rain has trickled." And Ritchie blushed.

It was one of those long and awkward journeys that eventually make you forget why you're on it. There were hold-ups in the tunnel under the Thames, and a just-missed Green Line gave them almost an hour to wait on the other side. During all of which the rain eased off and came back, stopped altogether and then started again, harder. And their conversation went the same way. They talked about this and that, then for short spells they dried up and looked around, and occasionally they hit on something which had the words pouring: cancer, families, school, racism. But as their clothes slowly dried so their reserve with each other evaporated as well: and while Ritchie had always easily been 'Ritchie', Sadie was now 'Sayd' without any awkwardness at all.

True to form, of course, the rain turned itself on for their getting off at Hornchurch Elms: but even with hoods up and heads down, they could see that they'd been dropped at the main road junction with a narrow street of small houses which led to a short row of shops. *The* Street: two pubs, a newsagent, a Co-op, a video shop, and a terrace of old country cottages.

With eyes all round them and mouths shut tight they walked the length of the empty street till they came out at the other end by a chapel with a crumbling porch. There they stopped and saw how the road further on narrowed to a country lane with the next house no more than a distant chimney. "What number?" Sadie asked.

"We passed it; I never said; number twelve, the one with the red curtains."

"And the geraniums?"

"Probably."

"So, what d'you reckon?"

Ritchie shrugged his shoulders, pulled her into the dry of the small porch. "I dunno. It's daft..." It was awkward confessing to thinking like a little kid. "I s'pose I hoped I'd see someone like him, sort of, getting into a car. You know..."

Sadie smiled. "That's not daft. Then he gets out again and spots you and asks how your dad is..."

"Be good, eh?" Ritchie smiled, too. Not much of a joke but it made him feel comfortable, coming from her.

"Well, you know where it is, so it won't need finding when you come back. An' it's good to picture where you'll be, in your mind, when you're psyching yourself up..."

"Yeah..." Although now he was here he didn't much

80

fancy walking up to that closed front door. The place looked every bit of the freezer he'd thought it would; the Blank House, with closed curtains and a front door shut as tight as sealed lips.

"Head up, Ritchie. You're not doing it for *you*. It's for your dad, remember? It's no fault of yours you're here." She was holding his hand suddenly, and squeezing some confidence into him. But what grabbed him was how well she'd read his mind, said the right thing. Yes, he was doing this out of love for his dad. If Lucy could be so worried about her dad that she'd ask awkward favours, then he could do the same, couldn't he? Especially off a relative, to save the man's life...

"Yeah," he said, "you're right." It was only a pity he'd have to be on his own when he did the asking.

They hurried down the street again, the rain sweeping in over the fields and forcing them to take in everything in a series of blinks, like an old film. But blink or stare there was still no sign of life at number twelve; and not much more at the shops. Only through the open door of one of the pubs, where a green screen of television sport suddenly looked like summer, did there seem to be anything going on at all. Ritchie looked back along the line of glistening slate to the corrugated roof which was the chapel. What a quiet old place. What a back of beyond. And was this the very street where his dad had grown up, where he'd come out to play, gone to the shops for his mum? Was this his dad's old territory; the place he'd lived longest in his life?

"Back on the bus then, Ritchie?" But Sadie's real request was to be let in on his thoughts. He had gone very quiet.

"Eh?"

"Going home?"

They were still outside the open door of the pub: and it was the sudden slam behind him which brought Ritchie back from where he'd been. A good slam. And a hand which grabbed hard at his shoulder, and shook it.

"What you doin' here, boy? What you doin' here? Don't

81

you know an answer when you get it?" The voice was deep but unbroken, a large female's. Ritchie spun with the hand holding on and helping in the twisting. It was a very big woman with angry eyes and a fast mouth demanding, "Eh? What you doin' over here?"

There was no room for doubt. He knew who this was. This was his Essex gran in all her fierceness.

"You. Come to see you." He managed to keep his voice from squeaking. "If you're..."

The woman still held him, looked at him at arm's length as if he were a coat she might or might not buy. "I'm Mrs Collins. But you're wasting your time, boy. And mine." She threw her head back at the pub. "I'm workin'. An' I'll tell you this once an' for all." She switched her angry look from Ritchie to the sky. "Come in here!" Tightening her grip she pulled him up the step and into the narrow doorway, brooking no argument. And he went with her, had no choice. The big woman frowned at Sadie. "An' her. Come on!"

Sadie followed into the small partitioned lobby of wood and glass.

"Now then!"

Out of the driving rain, Ritchie registered grey eyes, big features, thin gold leaves stapled through the ears and a small golden windmill on a chain round her neck.

"Your...mother...wasn't welcome in the week, boy, an' you ain't welcome now..."

Now Ritchie could see why his mother hadn't leapt at coming. What a mother-in-law! She was a *dragon*, this one.

"Skulking about like you was going for a walk in all this wet! What'd you think we are, country yokels? Recognised you, boy. Got your father's features." She clipped his ear but she was looking at his nose. "But don't think I'm comin' over all family. I done what I could for your father, gave your mother the use of the phone an' the numbers to ring. Past that I don't want to know – you got that clear?"

Her voice was loud enough for the public bar to hear, but no-one in there thought it odd enough to stop their own calling and laughing. Ritchie found himself nodding his head. She wasn't the sort you disagreed with. They'd had a cook at school like her, and the kids took a lot more notice of what she said than the Head.

"No good askin' me 'cos mine won't suit. That mother of yours should've told you that. If his sisters weren't good enough, that's the end of it. They can find someone else. Now –" There was a loud and dirty laugh behind her in the bar. She looked over her shoulder. She'd said what needed saying and that was that. She was going.

And even so, Ritchie couldn't find the words – or was it the guts? – to say the something that would keep her there till he'd got the answer to his question. Against this dragon he was in the sort of fright he'd be dead ashamed of afterwards.

"You can get back over the water an' don't let me see you no more!"

She was definitely going now. And still he couldn't say it.

Until a surprise hand quietly slipped into his: a cool squeeze of encouragement from Sadie O'Connell. And after a pause like a million years while the big woman stood there staring dislike at him, Ritchie somehow found the words and brought them out. "But what...about...his brother?" He was on his metal again, like standing up to Pearson. Sadie's nail dug in his palm. "That's who I've come looking for, if you want to know."

Like someone out of a late night film the big woman squared up to him and drew hard on the smoky air. But he stared her out, his legs like rhubarb, and she slowly began to nod, as if she were suddenly recognising that the boy knew something he shouldn't; the look of surprise when a child laughs at a joke aimed above his head.

"Oh, yes?" she said, quietly. "Oh, yes?"

He hadn't shocked her. And there was no way he had upset her by talking about someone who was dead, or in prison. It was him *knowing*: that was the look.

"Who's been letting cats out, then? Never *your mother!*"

83

She looked over her shoulder into the bar again. "Stay there! An' don't move." Turning very quickly for a big woman she disappeared into the drinking, left Sadie and Ritchie alone in the lobby, still holding hands.

"That changed her tune!" Ritchie said, dropping his hand. "Wonder what's..."

But she was back already, a blue reefer jacket held over her head like a hang glider; and with a rustle of blouse and the determination of a marine, she jerked her head for them to follow and ran across the teeming road to the door of number twelve. Heads down and splashing wet they ran after her, till they were indoors, too, and the door was shut.

"Give us those!" was the order. She grabbed their wet tops as they peeled them off and she took them out to the kitchen.

Precious seconds for a quick look round. Ritchie saw that they'd come into the living room straight from the street: there wasn't a hallway and only the kitchen led off from the small room, which meant that the stairs leading up to the bedrooms had to be out there somewhere. He noticed a small television set, one comfortable seat, a gas fire in a surround like the span of a bridge, a drop-leaf table and one straight-backed dining chair. Nothing he could see gave the room any feeling of belonging to anyone. It was like the temporary quarters he'd been in too many times. Except perhaps one picture by the mantelpiece; of a man frowning at the sun, one straight arm leaning on a sloping brick wall as if he were pushing it over. Otherwise the pictures were all scenes, with just one silver paper silhouette of an anchor in an oval black frame; and on the span of the mantelpiece a cheap blue windmill teapot with a matching sugar bowl and cream jug.

"He's not here then, is he? Satisfied? Looked under the table, have you?"

She must have been watching him from the kitchen. Ritchie said nothing at first, just stared back at her: but

84

she'd made him jump, and the jump had made him angry.

"It's not for me I want him, you know. It's for my dad." And she had spoken as if this uncle did exist. Ritchie was surprised by the strength of his own voice. "*Your son*, that's who it's for!"

"Oh, yes?" Her face had twisted up like a Pearson in the school yard. "Your father hasn't been my son for sixteen years, boy. So don't you come here with all that! I can't help you, nor don't bloody want to, neither!"

Something in Ritchie's gut twisted with the grip of an almost violent hate. He felt the hurt of the attack in his lips. But somehow what they said in reply came out quiet and controlled: persuasive. "See, his sisters weren't any good. They tried, but... And if there's a chance his brother might be a match..." Ritchie hunched his shoulders. "I'm trying everything, that's all."

Still her eyes refused to blink; but her muscles had relaxed and she looked more like a human being again. "They say it jumps a generation, don't they?" she asked; but more to herself than to him. "Anyhow, I still can't help you, boy. Billy don't come up any more; too busy with his business; an' I tell you, I wouldn't put you in touch with him if I could. Not for anything." She bent closer to him; and her breath was of peppermint, not drink. "Just you let sleeping dogs lie, you hear?"

"If you know where he is, you've *got* to tell me. Where is he? Eh? You've *got* to tell me..."

Slowly she shut her eyes in denial. "I s'pose you could advertise for him on the telly, like they do. But he won't come, boy. I know that one. He won't come, I know Billy. And he won't shed a tear, neither, I'll tell you that for nothing!"

"But if I just *asked* him..." Ritchie was pleading now.

And it did no good. A gust of wind hit the window like a slap round the face and the woman made a sudden move back to the kitchen. She came back with their tops and threw them hard into the wrong pairs of hands.

85

"Don't wheedle me, boy. Don't go trying to find no soft side in me because there ain't one. Now get off quick and take this girl with you, I got work to do!"

But mention of Sadie, the quick look at her, seemed to tip some balance with the girl. Up to then she'd been an observer; now she seemed drawn in by the vacuum of the big woman's unhelpfulness.

"We'll find him," she said, "if he's in business."

Gran Collins stopped with her hand up at her neck: no bluster for a second or two. Then she moved. Forcing Sadie to jump aside she strode across to the front door and let in the driving rain as she held it open.

"Go on, get off out of it. An' don't come back – you hear me?"

The knocker danced with the slam she gave the door. Ritchie fumbled into the awkward wet arms of his top; took the opportunity of his head being shielded to snatch a look at Sadie. How had she taken that? Did you say sorry for a hateful relative who treated you and your friend like dogs?

But Sadie didn't seem bothered: perhaps she'd seen a lot worse in her life. As her head came up she bent it left and right, tucked in her hair. "I'd like to beam her to China as a swap for my gran! Zap! Come on, *boy*, let's find that bus!"

She led off down the street, smiling and clutching his arm in some sort of excitement: dancing, almost.

But Ritchie wasn't dancing: he couldn't even take a step to asking Sadie what tune she'd suddenly heard. He couldn't get over that woman. He felt shell-shocked. What about someone who refused to help save the life of her own son? It was unbelievable: so much bad blood. What could have happened in the past to give her that hateful attitude? What terrible family secret was it that she couldn't shout it out at him in her anger? It was more than he could understand.

Sadie took his mood, shut up, stayed quiet for a bit while he went through it: till ten minutes later when they were wet through and uncomfortable and helping to steam up the windows of the next Green Line, she grabbed his hands in hers and rubbed them.

"Know what I think? Crazy shot – chance in a million?"

It took a second now for Ritchie to take his mind off her hands. "Yeah, go on..."

"What about windmills?" she asked. Now it was her eager eyes. "You ever seen so many in your life? Round her neck, on her mantelpiece, in those drawings. You see those drawings?" He had, and he hadn't. "All the same one, they were, all had three arms instead of four. All the same windmill." She looked round, looked back at him. "Or sails, are they? Anyway, a broken one, made a funny shape..."

Rising to her excitement now, Ritchie started nodding. "Yeah, I did see; only I was so bottled up I never noticed..." Although he had taken in the windmill pendant. These days he noticed anything worn round people's necks. "But who's to say that's his business...?" And then he remembered, quite clearly. The man leaning on the wall, the man who seemed to be pushing the wall over. "That photo ..." he said.

"Sloping. The bottom part of a windmill. They have tons in China, wooden ones. But they're the only sloping walls I know about..."

"And if that *was* him..." And didn't it have to be? It wasn't his dad, and the picture was too modern to be his grandad.

"See, her hands gave it away, too. Did you see? When she said he was too busy with his business they went straight to that thing round her neck. I know that touch. My mum does it when she talks about my gran: doesn't know she's doing it, but she always grabs at her locket..."

"Yeah! You're right!" What a great kid this was to invite herself along. What a stroke of luck...

"All the same windmill, they are, the one he's making his money out of. You find that an' I reckon you've found him!"

"Yeah..." But Ritchie turned away to see a domino line of tower blocks through the coach window. There were so many people in the world, and so many places to hide. Uncle Billy could be knocking out windmills in a garage *anywhere.*

"And a bit of sea in the corner; I had time to look."

"Cheers!" Ritchie gave her back her hands as the coach dropped them at the Blackwall Tunnel, to an easing of the rain for them to run to the 108 bus stop on the tunnel approach.

"An' there was something else. Something she said, about that Billy. I thought *hello* when she said it..."

"Yeah? What?" God, she'd been a find, this Sadie.

"Only it's gone. Can't think of it for the minute... Anyhow, we'll go looking for windmills, eh?" She clutched his arm with both hands, smiled at him, pressed herself enthusiastically to him in a smell of wet rain top: another sudden move which left Ritchie not sure whether to nod or shake his head. Because wouldn't it be good to be putting things straight somehow with Lucy, and doing the next bit of the search with her?

"See how I get on, eh?"

And as he found himself giving Sadie a squeeze in thanks, his inside rolled with the thought of how complicated life could be...

# CHAPTER SIX

The good news was, his dad was improving. Temporarily. The treatment was working. The report from the Sister when they went in on the Sunday was that the white cell count was returning to normal. Inside he was getting better. On the outside his hair was falling out – which didn't make him feel on top of the world: that, and being too sick to fancy his food, and too highly at risk from infection for him even to get a cuddle from June. But he *was* on the right track; he was responding: although – Sister's little joke, looking at his thinning head – this was the hairy time. An infected tooth could kill him.

The thing about the military was that they expected you to take in that sort of stuff like the news of a posting to Northern Ireland. Matter-of-fact and no argument. So they all knew how Dick was, Dick included. Good or bad, he'd always have to take it like a brave soldier. Which he had. But you can't obey an order to be cheerful, and that Sunday Dick was definitely down.

When Ritchie went in his dad put on a smile, but Ritchie saw the acting. Either parents can't act or their children are impossible audiences. Either way, it had Ritchie feeling bad about wanting the visiting time to go fast; time filled with trivial talk about this and over-done enthusiasm about that: cricket scores and videos and the Isle of Man T.T.; but he did want to get away, and badly.

He was determined to get to his mother's handbag. Sadie's windmill discovery was all very well, he reckoned, and he'd spent a lot of time going over all the ways anyone could run a souvenir business, but other things had happened over at Hornchurch Elms, and other things been said.

And some of them concerned his mother. Was he dreaming it or making it up, or did he get the feeling that Gran Collins had been saying his mother knew more than she let on? And if so, what was it? Could she be carrying some clue which the windmill knowledge could make clear: a letter or something which could give a reason for the bad blood?

He'd never been the sort to dip into his mother's handbag; and she'd never been the sort to be all top-of-the-wardrobe about it. For as long as he could remember the handbag had been here, there and everywhere – including lost. And he'd be sent to get something out of it as naturally as if it were a drawer in the living room. But seeing his dad suffer – however bravely and in response to the drugs – was something he couldn't bear. He was going to find that brother, whatever trust he broke, and wherever he had to root around.

And he knew what his best chance at the handbag would be. After that afternoon's visiting, on the one day of the week when June could still be normal. Whatever else she did that Sunday she would do her exercises and then she would have her bath. Old June looked all right for a mother, turned a few heads when she went down the street, made sure mirrors paid for themselves. She was the one who, at family days, always had the officers making sure she was all right for a cup of tea. What she called the pot belly on her had about as much bump as an ironing board, and she could still embarrass Ritchie with no bra in the summer. All of which she worked hard at: diet, skin care and exercises followed by a long, hot bath. Which was when the handbag would be his, when he had found it.

The pair of them were in a state of truce; had simply stopped talking about a donor – because although each of them knew best, they weren't going to get the other one going by saying so. She was all for the Anthony Nolan Register now. He wanted to test that brother. But the talk was all about how his dad looked and what the Sister said, and food and shirts and *EastEnders*. For all either of them

90

said, Billy Collins might as well never have been born.

He found the handbag in the kitchen, on the tall stool next to the fridge. June had run from her bedroom to the bath: and at the click of the bolt Ritchie was halfway out of his chair. The trouble was, he really needed an accomplice. He could just have done with Sadie there to help him again, watching the bathroom for signs of his mother coming out while he was at the handbag. Or Sunil, or someone – it didn't have to be Sadie. . . But it was on his own, with the pulse at his neck thumping hard, that Ritchie made his move. After one last nervous run back to look at the bathroom door, he unclipped the black bag and delved into its soft skiver belly, his fingers manouevring, his eyes alert for a piece of paper, a letter, a small notebook – anything which might give him some clue to the mystery. He was so jumpy he had to force himself to concentrate on what he was seeing. His fingers were shaky and clumsy: imagine being Bomb Disposal in a state like this! Coins, ballpoint pens, nail file, compact, hair clips and cheque book; car keys on a fob, a biscuit in a tissue, some fivers in a pocket, and a fine layer of escaped powder over everything; with a couple of local till receipts, a broken ear-ring and some Barry August business cards. This was what he rummaged among, all this and a bottle of nail varnish: but there wasn't a notebook or a diary, or an envelope, and no little pieces of paper. He'd drawn a blank; and he was certain of that.

Saying something obscene he carefully rearranged the bag to be as careless as he'd found it, and, starting to breathe again, he nipped for another look at the bathroom door.

And it was then that his concentration went for a vital second. The big bag tipped slightly on the stool – and the nail varnish slid out hard and heavy to crack on the tiles of the kitchen floor.

"What was that?"

His mother had ears like bats' radar. And look at the mess on that floor!

"Nothing. Dropped something, no sweat. . ."

91

But she was finished and coming out. He could hear water rushing to get to the waste. And the pool on the kitchen floor was like some blood sample, thickening, with so many bits of thick glass held in it there was no quick wipe up, either. All the same, Ritchie panicked at it with a rip of paper towel, found how nail varnish sticks like glue.

"What the hell are you doing? Ritchie Collins! What's all this?"

He was crouching there like a murderer at the scene. Discovered, with a tell-tale stain in the grouting.

"You've been down my bag! You little *toe-rag!*"

A smack round the head might have come next: except she never hit him.

"What you after? Eh? Eh?"

Ritchie gave up the half-hearted wiping. He stood and faced her, saw her hands trembling as they clutched the kimono angrily around, her turban tight enough to swell her red face.

"Sorry, Mum. Thought you'd picked up my calculator by mistake..."

She stared. Didn't believe. Wasn't brought up on a winkle barge.

"Money, is it? You want money? You've got money enough in your Post Office! Have we ever kept you short of money?" She went for the bag and pulled out one of the fivers, thrust it at him, threw it. "I'm *disgusted!*"

And then she had it. It might have been a coincidence, looking down again at the coagulating floor, but she had it.

"Oh! *Uncles*, is it? *Clues*? It's not bloody money at all! It's you being right!" she screeched. "And me and your dad being wrong!"

"No..."

"Of course! Of course! Huh!" She turned on her bare heel and went off to the living room, threw herself into an armchair, hunched there, started rocking like a disturbed child. "Oh, yes..."

Ritchie followed her in; slowly, awkwardly.

92

"Leave it!" she shouted at him. "Got that, leave it, will you?" She jumped up again, went to the television, took something from under the lid of a small steel duck. "I thought those sodden clothes had some story to tell! Showing London to a little girl friend! You were over Essex, weren't you? Little wet bus tickets, Sunshine!"

She waved them at him, and he blinked. She *was* sharp.

"I tell you, Ritchie Collins, drop it! It won't work, not from either end, it won't. May and Eileen didn't want to be pushed on where he is, and Special Branch wouldn't get it out of Gran Collins. He wouldn't come and your father wouldn't have him, so *leave it*, do you hear?" She was walking round the room, one hand to her kimono, the other picking up ornaments and putting them down again. "They're going to come up with a perfect donor, so leave it, you hear?"

Ritchie didn't bother to argue. They were past all that. He knew what the different chances were better than she did, he had inside information, and all he wanted was the best. But if she couldn't see it, he wasn't going to convince her. Only coming up with his Uncle Billy would do that – because then the M.O. would also have something to say about the best chance, wouldn't he? So he retreated to the kitchen and took some Ajax to the tiles.

Anyway, it was all out in the open now. The race.

Furiously, he went at the grouting with a nail brush; but the mark, he knew, would be stuck in there for ever. Even with solvent there'd be traces: and they'd see it, it would remind them about today until for one reason or another they moved out of the flat.

To their little business on the A22, God willing: all three of them.

Ritchie's dream machine was bigger than the bikes they used in the displays. It was still a Suzuki, but the 750cc model, the one on the front of May's *Motorcycle Sport* which could double on road and circuit, and was flash enough to turn heads wherever it went. Especially right now, as Ritchie, in midnight blue leathers, took the one correct line for the ninety degree left hand corner on the Green Line route to Hornchurch Elms.

This was the only way to do it, he thought; this was how you got round the country looking for a windmill with three sails.

He hadn't got undressed for ages after the business over the handbag. There was homework he should have done – when wasn't there? – but he'd pushed that back into its folder. He should have had a wash and cleaned his teeth before bed, but he hadn't; he'd preferred to lie there with his eyes closed, overtaking a line of army vehicles in convoy, roaring past the outriders on the crown of the road with the bike's ridged wheels biting at the central white line.

As he rode he could still hear the slide and bang of drawers and cabinets in her room next door, could still imagine her mind racing with her own fast moves to get the hospital chasing to find a donor.

He leant forward into the petrol tank and took the fly-over across the next junction, open-throttling up the display ramp. Below him, the Green Line was having to go round the slow way, till suddenly he was above it, leaping buses – brave and fast and safe as houses with his skilled hands. He leapt over Sadie in the coach the way the Red Helmets went over cars, and he had a hand to spare to wave down at her in one of the windows; recognised the shining bare shoulder.

And who was that driving the coach, without the hair?

Gripping hard, arms fighting, Ritchie twisted the brakes and sent the bike into a long, controlled skid along the road. He was getting off, he didn't like this any more. He wasn't so deeply asleep he couldn't stop when he wanted. But he was out of breath as he came properly to, and he had to quieten himself to listen to his mother's bedroom next door. Had he imagined the click of her light switch?

No, he definitely hadn't liked that last bit. Sadie and the

94

shoulder, well, all right, although of course it should've been Lucy. But his dad, up there driving...with two hands on the steering wheel which were no more than skeleton bones...

He shivered; got in under the bed clothes and curled up in the foetal position, refused to see those eyes in their dead stare at the road ahead, so different from the sharp face in its helmet. Instead he tried to force something pleasant into his head, something good to cling on to...but as the minutes clicked on and on he came to the awful discovery that sometimes there just isn't anything. Sometimes there's nothing in the world to cheer; nothing on earth to want to stay awake for any more. He tried some safe bets from the past – trips, holidays, something new to wear, the Suzuki he was really saving for; but what were all those now? Nothing! And that brilliant feeling he'd had of seeing Lucy at school – enough to turn him over a few days ago – that was just pathetic now, seeing how wrong the whole thing had gone.

No, there wasn't anything: and he could feel his eyes shrivel in his head, his mouth set itself in a down. So, was this when people did it, he wondered? Was this when people took their own ways out of the real world?

He shuddered, sat up. Come on, he wasn't having that! He looked around in the dark, widened his eyes as if he were making an answer to someone. That wasn't the way enemies got beaten, wars got won, was it? That wasn't his dad's way. His dad's way was, you fought it. You reconnoitred it, you drew up your plans and you *fought* it.

Like he was fighting for his dad, like he was determined to find that brother...

And so why wasn't he fighting for Lucy, too? His back straightened. What was he doing giving in, letting her think what she wanted to about his Saturday with Sadie? What the hell was wrong with him, not putting her straight about all there was between him and the new girl?

Why didn't he *tell her*? Just tell her? If she didn't believe him, that was something else: but he could at least talk to her, couldn't he, instead of acting so pathetic?

The idea was so blessed obvious he wondered why he hadn't thought just to tell her before. What sort of tail-between-the-legs mood had let her go off on Friday with all the wrong ideas? When all it was about was him sticking up for Sadie O'Connell and her helping him back? There wasn't any more to it than that, was there? So why not just say so, if Lucy was supposed to be so special?

He lay back down again. Which she was; oh yes, she definitely was! This time he stretched himself in the bed, forgot the curling up in the womb and sprawled instead, took himself to Greenwich Park, the Common. And cursed himself for being such an idiot. Of course he'd tell her tomorrow, first thing: just watch him!

Sunil caught him first, made a close inspection of the healing face, tried to make some plans but Ritchie stayed evasive. And then Sadie found him, but he didn't get too uptight. After all, she was only an ordinary friend, he was going to explain all this... But she was very excited; and was there something different about her again?

"I nearly phoned you last night." Her words were pitched on top of one another so fast they almost sounded like a different language. "Ritchie, you know I said she'd said something special, your gran, and then I couldn't think of it...?" Her skin seemed stretched tight with the importance of what she'd got to tell him. "Something my dad said an' I remembered, Ritchie, I remembered the words..." Her eyes flashed in the sun. "In her house. She said, 'Billy doesn't come up any more' – something like that; you remember now?"

Ritchie nodded. "She did say something like that..." But he couldn't quote word for word, he'd been in too much of a state with the fierce old woman to take any notes...

"Well, it's important, I think."

And her face said she really thought it was. She was on to something.

"See, I've been listening to everyone talking. It's what you do, coming back after you've been away. And what does everyone say? I can hear it. *Up* to London, they say, and *down* to the country; or the seaside. Isn't that right, Ritchie, eh?"

He nodded. "Yeah..." It was — and he could see what she was driving at.

"See, if he came *up* to see your gran at that place — Hornchurch Elms — he must've come from somewhere further...sort of, *down*." She waved her arms, laughed, scratched her nose. "Have I got that right?"

"Dead right!"

"It wasn't *over*, was it — which could've been Germany or Hong Kong? An' it wasn't *down* from Scotland or London. So you see what I mean, it narrows it a bit, doesn't it?"

"It does. Yeah..." She was sharp, too, this Sadie. Sharp as his mum...

"Down by the sea somewhere. South coast. A windmill with three sails."

"If it's a real windmill, not made up..."

"But if it *is*, like the drawings look — it'll give us something to go on for half-term, won't it?"

Ritchie wasn't so sure about the 'we': but leave it. "Yeah, there might be someone near who knows where they make all the souvenir stuff. Might be a little shop..."

"It's a start, eh?"

"It's a good start. Cheers, Sayd!"

"That's all right." Just for a second she looked as if she wanted to say more; but she didn't, just kept the eye contact: and *now* he could see how she was different today. She was wearing the faintest line of make-up to bring out the special shape of her eyes, had put it on the way June did hers, with a very fine brush.

It was a two fingers sort of sign for the Pearsons of the world. And very pretty, too.

"Can't wait. Got to go. See you." Ritchie ran across the yard to perform a quick pretence in the outside lavatory. He did need to buy some time to get to Lucy, if he could. He did deserve today going just a bit his way, he reckoned.

The fates must have agreed, because somehow all the good things did happen. Sadie O'Connell coming up with that other clue had only been the start. Homework wasn't called in till he'd got enough copied off Sunil to see him through: and, best of all, Lucy didn't run away when he went up to her. She was ready to hear him out: meet him halfway, even.

Well, so much for giving up on everything, he thought. So much for wanting to take a dive...

He caught her just right; he came rushing out of the lavatories and there she was coming in through the gate: smiling, pretty, looking her old self. He didn't beat about the bush. He ran straight over to her before she got to anyone else and called her, asked her for two minutes of her time. "Only two minutes..."

Serious herself now, weight on one foot, she looked him in the eye. "Two minutes? I'm not rushing anywhere..." And right there, ignoring everyone coming in past them – Tony, Sunil, Des Banks and Mrs Ross – just pulling her a bit to one side, he told her everything. Absolutely everything. About Mr O'Connell's job, all the business over donors, and Sadie's offer to help – what Saturday had really been about. He even got in about the Essex dragon and the windmill with three sails. He started, got going, and spelt it all out for her as if he were someone helping the police with their enquiries, because there wasn't going to be the faintest shadow of any doubt between them. At the end of it all she shifted her weight and squinted at him in the sun.

And she smiled. "So you never want to see me again?"

"No!" Ritchie had thrown a hand in his hair in exasperation before he realised he was being wound up. "You know I do! I want to see you again...a lot. Otherwise...Strewth, I wouldn't have bothered with all this grovel..."

Lucy looked at her feet. "Anyhow cheers for bothering. I

98

didn't think you could be all that, over...*her*." She wrinkled up her nose. "When, then? Wednesday? No evening visiting, Wednesday: it's a bit the same for me as it is for you, hospital and that. What about Wednesday, then?"

"Yeah, Wednesday's all right!"

"You're not chasing off anywhere with Suzie Wong?"

Ritchie swallowed it, let it go. "No. I'll be around."

"Pray for sun, then!"

"Pray for sun!"

"Greenwich Park?"

"Sounds all right to me."

And that was that. He'd cracked it. She'd heard him out and she'd understood.

A different day to yesterday, he thought!

It might have been part of his routine or it might have been special, but Colonel Blake was on the ward that night, walking slow and talking fast, the way doctors do in a crisis. But he took time out to come and give a few words of encouragement to Ritchie and his mother.

"Good news, then," he said. Ritchie held his breath. "The treatment's working, we're very pleased with him, there's a fair chance we'll have him in complete remission and home within the month if he keeps this progress up." He cranked on a smile, and then nodded his head to give them a chance to react.

At least the good news hadn't been about a donor yet. It was June who sighed. "Any other news, sir? Anything from the Register?"

The M.O. stood up straight. "Oh, no; but then they'd have surprised me if they had, just yet. Computer time, and all that. But not to fret, not to fret. From the day he walks out of here in remission we shall have a full six months to find someone. A full six months. So we've got no worries on that score, no worries at all..." Now he did inspect his toecaps. "It was a shame about the sisters, but, as I say, not to fret at all. Like the mounties, we always

99

get our man. Usually. Now..." The top man excused himself, went back to a huddle with an assistant by the drugs cupboard.

Six more months! Well, that was something. Time enough to look at every windmill in the south of England if he wanted to. But time for the Register to do its stuff, too...

June said nothing, wouldn't look at him; instead they went over together to start smiling at Dick Collins, ready to tempt him with some boned chicken; in the hope the poor bloke could keep it down.


The park was different of an evening. There weren't the tourists sauntering all over, only the joggers being determined, the dog-walkers pretending their dogs weren't theirs, and a few people who knew the quiet spots and disappeared like camouflage. The Observatory was shut and, being ahead of Wimbledon fortnight, the tennis courts were only painted lines and sagging nets. All these acres of park for around fifty people: Salisbury Plain was probably more populated: and that was nice, Ritchie thought, it was like a walk in the country.

This time he and Lucy went there together, met at the NAAFI and walked.

The weather was good again; but the mood between them more polite, somehow. There wasn't the teasing of that Saturday at the fête: and Lucy hadn't worn the ribbon Ritchie liked. It was like finding their way again through a lot of talk about their fathers, swapping latest news. And they didn't hold hands on the way. As they went, though, the talk livened up, and by the time they got to the big gates there was quite a bit of laughing going on, till Lucy asked him if it was true Tony was getting a car next birthday. But he didn't get too upset. She had to talk to people, didn't she? She wasn't in a nunnery. Going from kissing the way you didn't tell your mother to ignoring each other for a couple of days, it was only natural he'd find the first half

100

hour a bit strange... At least he still felt fairly confident about bringing his St. Christopher along with him.

Anyway, weren't things down to him as well? Why should he always expect her to say and do the right things? So while the shadow of the park gate was still across their shoulders he took her hand and squeezed it, the way Sadie did. And Lucy squeezed back; question and answer.

"Which way?" he asked. "Want to see the power station again?" He wondered if they'd find the dent in the ground they'd found before.

"Let's have a look at the view, eh?"

"Yeah, good idea." But it was the famous view she meant, the public one, where you stayed on the path and carried on towards the Observatory, and the statue of General Wolfe looked down at the Queen's House and the Naval College and the river: not the view from their private place.

Never mind. Girls had awkward times, had different moods. At least they were back together again.

When they got there Lucy leaned on the railing and looked out over the river without a word: took it in and turned away. "Oh, yeah, the meridian," she said. "Almost forgot the meridian was here." She was pointing to where the zero degree line was painted on the Observatory wall and let into the path, the physical evidence of the line drawn on the map.

Ritchie acted some interest. "Oh, yes." And he led her over to it.

"There!" Lucy planted a foot firmly on each side. "A foot in each hemisphere. East, west, home's best."

Ritchie stood behind her, planted a foot on each side, too; put his arms round her waist. "East, west, Lucy's best," he said softly.

"That's what they say..."

She wriggled, and they laughed. This was more like Greenwich Park.

"Is this true north or is it magnetic?" A middle-aged couple with a guide book had come up and wanted to be

101

technical: certainly weren't going to stand astride the line like tourists. Leading the way, Ritchie walked Lucy further round the path where the grass sloped, facing the reddening rays of the sun.

It was still a public place, this, and they weren't as relaxed as before; but they didn't talk about their fathers. After a while, freeing a hand from the press of the grass, Ritchie shifted and went for the chain of his St. Christopher: watched her closed eyes as he pulled the medallion up to his throat.

She squinted in the sun and saw what he'd moved for. And, "No," she said, pushing it back, "you keep it, Ritch..."

"Eh?" Ritchie felt the flush of embarrassment tingle on his face as his stomach turned in disappointment. "Why not?"

"Just...you know...it's not necessary." Lucy sat up, crossed her legs at the ankles. "You don't have to wear special things, not at our age..."

"No, sure." He dropped it back down his neck, quick as a hanging. So why the change? "I just thought..."

Lucy got up, made a big thing of pulling him up after: and Ritchie let it take its time, because once on his feet they'd walk left or right, and he had to make up his mind. He'd brought some money to go down to the *Plume of Feathers* and chance looking eighteen. Or, it wouldn't be too early to walk back home.

They walked back home: slowly, and with Lucy holding his hand tight. She put her head against his for part of the way, and spoke in a soft voice: and when they got to the flats they kissed goodnight and looked forward to their next date, and to all the hassles of school, just the way they had before.

But it was different this time. Tonight the St. Christopher felt not so much like silver round Ritchie's neck, as lead.

"You know where I was last night?" Sadie O'Connell caught up with Ritchie in the corridor.

102

It was only nine o'clock. Too early for all this *I-saw-you* business. "No? Where?"

"Down the library. And guess what I found, Ritchie?"

"Give in!"

"This!" She whipped a book from out of her bag, a touch of magic in the jostle; a thin book with a stapled cover and a picture of a windmill on the front. *Windmills.*

"Hey! It hasn't got..." He leant back against the wall and let everyone surge past him.

"Got our windmill? What do you want for your money? But..." She took the book back from him and turned it over, pointed to an address on the cover. "'The British Windmill Society'. It gives the address. They might know it, eh?"

"They might... Yeah, can't be that many..." She made him feel neglectful. He hadn't even started the real planning of finding the windmill, outside his stupid Suzuki and blue leathers dream; he'd been too busy out in the park...

Tonight, though, he'd been going to think about it, and he knew next week was half-term and he could have whole days out while June was at work. "Can I borrow this for a bit?"

"Course you can. It's *for* you."

"Right. Cheers, Sayd. See you later, eh?"

He deliberately didn't watch her go but read the address on the book cover instead: he was still aware of eyes that might be looking, blue eyes he reckoned he might still need to convince.

In an empty room, at a desk in full view of the door — always a safe place to choose when you were dodging a lesson — Ritchie went thoroughly through the windmills book, read it very carefully, turned the pictures about, screwed up his eyes to blur the black and white photographs to be like the drawings. Did any of them look like the one? He wished he could go back and give them some attention now instead of being told his fortune by that old dragon. All right, all these windmills had four sails, but the book wasn't exactly new, and a sail could have come to grief since, couldn't it? It was the background he needed. A bit of land and a corner of sea. Which several of them had: mills in Kent, Sussex, and Norfolk.

He shut the book, took a look at the back cover again. 'The British Windmill Preservation Society, 10, Ruddles Square, London, N1.' Sadie was right. There was a society, so they might know, mightn't they? That was if the dragon's drawings hadn't just been made up, done on the kitchen table...

He looked at his watch, worked out some times: and decided he could count on a good half hour on his own if he hurried home fast. Half an hour of the phone to himself before June came in.

If Lucy was surprised at the speed they went home, she didn't show it. They didn't hang about: kept to the foot-path, and talked about all sorts except windmills. He surprised himself, not sharing his plans with her, not roping her in for half-term already, and he didn't know why. Perhaps it would take too long to explain and time was short right now. Certainly all he could see was that phone at home, and that windmill with three sails... Anyhow, Lucy seemed to understand. She wasn't for pulling him off to see any castles today, either.

The British Windmill Preservation Society was a pretty small affair, Ritchie found. The man who answered the phone was the one who was prepared to help him, and when it sounded as if a visitor had walked into his office, he offered to phone Ritchie back.

"Cheers, but haven't got much time today." The last thing Ritchie wanted was a call back. Imagine June picking it up. "I could ring you back tomorrow."

"As you wish. I'll dig out some recent reports. We do rely on members' reports, you know, for the current state of standing mills." His voice slowed as he wrote on: "A three-sailed tower mill by the sea, Southern Counties..."

"Or Eastern. Like, Clacton, you know. Thanks. It's just

104

this exam work I'm doing..." Could Ritchie hear the car? "I'll ring you tomorrow. A bit earlier, probably..." He'd miss games. Grow a verruca, get home and give himself more time.

It wasn't June: as it turned out he had another half hour, time to hide the windmill book away, prick a couple of large potatoes for the oven and flick through the *Motorcycle News* he'd stepped over on the mat: even had time to spread his Geography homework over the coffee table.

But he really got down to Land Mass and Weather when his mother came in.

He heard the front door go, listened for the usual sounds of the arrival. Shoes off, *clump*, *clump*; the swish of the jacket on the bed; followed by crackling through into the living room with the stuff for the kitchen: Lean Cuisine or a fresh chop. Today, though, after just a bit longer than usual, she came in and stood facing him.

"Wotcha!" He looked up from his isobars, smiled – the good old Ritchie. Her shirt was a bit damp at the armpits, her face straight and uncool.

"So what's all this about windmills, then?"

Ritchie almost looked down to check his flies, it was that sort of feeling. The book was where she wouldn't find it in his bed, the thought was where she couldn't see it in his head. So how the devil had she got on to his secret?

"What d'you mean?" The man hadn't phoned back, he'd have heard the bell; besides which, he hadn't given the number. And Sadie knew about keeping quiet about all this.

"Windmills. Joined some *preservation* society, have you?" She walked through with some food to the kitchen.

"Do what?" Play along. He didn't know *how* she knew, but know she did, so play along. "Only school. Des Banks. One of his new exam options – Energy. Might do it. Fossil, solar, nuclear...wind...you know..." He got up and followed her into the kitchen. "Why, you met him?" A good stroke. "Thought you were a bit late."

"No." She'd lost her edge, softened as she ran some steak

under the tap. "I went to use the phone and did what I'm doing all day at bloody Barry August. Hit the redial button. I'm tired!" She ran a hand wearily through the hair. "Got some windmill society!" She managed a laugh. "Good job it wasn't one of your lady loves!"

"Yeah." Ritchie got out of the kitchen. "Silly old you!"

But June Collins didn't reply. By now she was taking something out on the steak, giving it a good bashing.

It was like you do in judo, turning the force of your opponent to your own advantage. Ritchie told his dad about the energy project, and talked to him about windmills as enthusiastically as if they were motorbikes; he even got in some talk of going to see one working somewhere.

"Your camera, Dad. The Nikon. Reckon I could borrow it, half-term? We can use photographs and everything in the new exam..."

But while he was using this ploy on his poor old dad, Ritchie's nerve-endings were more attuned to how June was reacting: after all, she'd been to Hornchurch Elms and might have seen the pictures; she might be trying to keep one step ahead for some reason. But she didn't react. (Not forgetting for a second that she was a brilliant actress, and sharp. Look at that last number redial stunt she'd pulled.) Even so, after Ritchie's initial flurry, it was Dick Collins who took the attention.

He was a very sick man. Colonel Blake and the Sister might be pleased with his progress, the drugs could be working and he was already on the road to a remission: but he was going through hell on the way, anyone could see that. Ritchie always went off before his mum and dad had their private talk, so they thought they were keeping the worst of it from him – the pain, the depression, the being sick and the bleeding from nasty places, the wanting to roll over and die. But Ritchie guessed at a lot of it. *Champion*, that film about the jockey who beat cancer, didn't pull the punches on what these drugs did to you while getting better

106

was going on. And when his dad said he could do what he wanted with the camera – the camera whose lens he stroked with a soft brush and put away in polystyrene at the back of a cupboard – then Ritchie knew how rough he was.

Lending the camera to him was almost like leaving a will...

"Cheers, Dad. I'll take care of it."

"Course you will." And the man had gone back to closing his eyes, like staring at the ceiling through the transparent lids.

Changes happened daily. And today's change was him not putting on an act for the visitors any more.

Ritchie crackled in his plastic apron and looked at his mother's eyes above her mask. He raised his eyebrows. But her stare back at him was as sharp as ever.

# CHAPTER SEVEN

The windmill, the man reckoned, was at Potton Head — the tower mill he wanted with a broken sail. But he was awfully sorry — it probably wouldn't help him much in his exam. The structure had lost its old wooden machinery when people had moved in, and lean-to's had been added on with no feeling for history. There were better examples elsewhere without going down into that corner of Essex.

"Essex? It is Essex, then?"

"Foulness Island, out past Southend: near the gun ranges. But I can give you several others..."

It wasn't shown on the Ordnance Survey. Ritchie checked quietly, in his bedroom. Potton Head itself was, one of those map references with three houses and a road so minor it was left in white. But there was no sign of a windmill because it wasn't preserved — according to Sadie's book. At least the place wasn't very big, Ritchie thought. People would know it. You might have trouble finding a Saxon well, but not a great big windmill. And if it was out past Southend — well, Southend was easy, wasn't it?

Ritchie refolded the map.

What would have been great would be to go and find it the way he had in the dream: in a new set of leathers on his Suzuki, with Lucy up behind. But he was a few months short of any of that. He threw the map up onto a shelf. It'd be train and bus for him, an all day job. Find the windmill, then talk to locals till he got a line on the souvenir business he reckoned Billy Collins ran.

At least money was no problem. He had a Giro account which they topped up on birthdays and, with a bike lined up for his next one, he hadn't been the biggest of spenders recently. He could get all he needed and more over the Post Office counter.

No, the real hassle was going to be time, the actual *when* of going; because June Collins was sharp and he wouldn't blind her with a bit of wool pulled over the eyes. No way. She could spot a dodgy story with her head still under the pillow. This one had to be really clever.

Either really clever, or the truth! Why not? Ritchie's eyes fixed on the thought as if it were something he could see coming at him from a long way off. Stupid! Of course! Be like the agents in half the spy books he read. Didn't they *live* their cover? They didn't pretend to be something, they *were* it, weren't they? They wouldn't have pretended to be researching into windmills, they'd have been doing it for real – writing books about it.

Good thought, Ritchie told himself. One of the units of his Economics could really be on power; and with talk of harnessing the wind as a part answer to the nuclear thing, why not look at various examples of the past: work out their levels of efficiency? He could at least get close to a few of them – and he wouldn't go red telling his mum about chasing some windmill when it was the third one that week! Not that windmills meant anything to her. He was sure of that by now. Whatever she was sitting on, it wasn't knowing about Billy Collins and his souvenirs. They'd have had World War Three after the redial business if she knew anything about that side of things.

Excited now, and pleased with himself, Ritchie read the windmill book from cover to cover. He made notes, copied diagrams, did a couple of sketches of different designs of sails – and he started to leave one or two about. He wanted to shake his own hand when he got told to blow his windmill things off the dining table: and he did a little dance at having cracked it when she moved some off herself without a second look.

Getting interested, he started on an essay; and picking a location from Sadie's book, he made serious arrangements to get over to the mill on Wimbledon Common on the Monday, all of which he made sure to discuss with June. And on the day, he put a film in his dad's best camera and he went. A day of half-term, and the opening section of his essay. 'Sail strength and energy: is maintenance the only overhead?'

Of course, it was closed. Windmills usually are. But it was his first experience of standing under those giant arms, feeling small: and by the time he'd sketched and photographed and re-read the bit in the book about keeping the sails balanced or pay the cost in repairs, he could think about Potton Head and its three sails without his heart rate speeding. His Economics unit was why he was going there: and he was almost prepared to believe it. His cover was getting very good.

But certain other thoughts were still getting his pulse going all right. Lucy was being very nice again, and they went over to Jack Woods on the Monday evening before visiting and had a lean against a tree to remember. But it really only heightened his feeling of disappointment at how special this half-term week could have been. Unfortunately, with his plans ("*Windmills?* Do us a favour, Ritchie!") and some of hers which she didn't go into, sorting out other days to be alone was difficult, and they had to leave it.

Anyhow, *she* had bought it. June. She didn't look at him with pointed eyes when he mentioned windmills; and she even brought it up as something to say during one of their difficult visits to Ritchie's demoralised dad. And, without being too specific about where, he took off without question for the windmill he wanted on the Wednesday – the day he wouldn't need to be back for an evening visit.

It was lonely. Without Sadie it was definitely lonely this time. There were plenty of people about because Southend at the summer half-term was a big attraction, plenty of families on the train, and even an old couple in the carriage – her feeding him with sandwiches as if he were some big baby – which had Ritchie thinking sadly how different his

110

family was right now. Once in the salt and vinegar of Southend, though, he started feeling a bit different. He stared-out one of a pair of girls who went past (and she looked back over her shoulder); his Levi 501's fitted well, and he reminded himself of the cool way he'd set this visit up. What was more, he could well be quite close to Billy Collins: could even have passed him in the street already. Cheap windmill souvenirs seemed just about the mark down here. His hand went to the camera case. Southend could be L.A., he could be C.I.A., ready to jump his man or melt into the nearest bar . . .

Which seemed an excellent idea. It was hot, and he looked eighteen, didn't he? But he decided against. He'd got a job to do: find a windmill and then track down a few souvenirs and the man who knocked them out. He could have a drink later. To celebrate, please God!

The single-decker to Potton Head was a Southend Transport 4a, with one of those driver/conductors who'd only be really happy at a funeral. You could see him being next best thing to a week of rain for taking the edge off anyone's holiday.

"Potton Head? Caravan site. You ask for Droy's Caravan Site. Thirty pence."

"But is that Potton Head?"

"It's Droy's Caravan Site on my timetable. That's the proper way to ask the driver." And the man practically pushed him on into the bus in order to scowl at a young woman bulged out with shopping. "How many seats you want to pay for?"

And the drive was all twist and discomfort. They seemed to stop more than they went, touring every small group of houses on the estuary. The bus windows were spattered with mud, and Ritchie's eyes began to ache with the squint of seeing out. Also, it wasn't the best of mystery journeys for suddenly remembering he'd needed a pee before he started. Urgently, he looked all about for the three sails of the windmill: but all he could see was a lot of hedge, huge

111

tracts of half grown cereal, and long, dividing dykes. The bus vibrated at its long stops by the white-board houses and the general shops, and when it was going they seemed to be travelling round in circles on some endless landscape, an unreal world where Ritchie would never again see anything he recognised.

With the vibration of the bus Ritchie's personal need to get off was just becoming painful when the next row of houses ran up to a sea wall, and there, with a spiteful spin of his wheel, the driver lurched the bus to a halt and switched off his engine.

Relieved, but still sweating and having to give it a few seconds before standing up, Ritchie followed everyone off.

It was Droy's Caravan Site all right. The sign across the roadway leading in said so; and hiding behind a paved sea wall like creatures sheltering in its lee were rows of small caravans, soft tyred in the grass.

Ritchie saw them from the step: but he couldn't summon even a jump from the bus. He was hot, uncomfortable and dispirited, back to feeling the way he had on the train.

Come on! How would his dad be doing if he gave in like this?

Taking in a deep breath of estuary air, Ritchie looked about him: and didn't know how the flat views from the bus could have hidden it! There it was, about half a mile away to the west on a piece of high ground, sticking up for the world to see. The windmill. And it was definitely the one. It was the three sailed windmill in the pictures without a shadow of any doubt.

Excited again, Ritchie twisted around and ran to the kiosk at the entrance to the caravan park, where a woman behind the glass was reluctant to leave a line she was adding to look up.

"Excuse me," he interrupted, "that windmill. Have you got any souvenirs of it, please?"

The woman shook her head, keeping her eyes steady on her line of figures. "No, don't sell things here."

112

"But do they do souvenirs of it? Teapots and that?"

Still the figures went tapping onto the calculator. "It's the shop you want."

"Yeah? Where's the shop?"

"Down there on your left. Site shop. But shut Wednesdays. Early closing."

"Oh! Any other shops?"

"Wakering. Dunno what they've got."

Ritchie really hated this woman by now: sitting there in her fag smoke, looking like all the women he'd ever seen taking money on fairground rides, and sod the world.

"Back on that bus, is it?"

"Not that one."

Well, he wasn't going to ask the driver. He'd find someone else. Or get up there to that windmill and talk to the owner. He might not want it preserved, but he'd know about the souvenirs, that was for sure.

Everything else forgotten, Ritchie set off on a fast walk along the sea wall. The breeze blew in the sounds of sea birds he didn't know and container ships he couldn't see, till he reached shelter down a ramp and took a narrow road between two hedges. Then a steepish pull for forty or fifty metres up to the gate of the mill yard, and the sign.

BARLING'S MILL. PRIVATE ROAD. NO ENTRY. And pinned by the side of it a picture of an alsatian with an *I live here* warning.

There was no sign of the dog, and no sound. But things weren't always what they seemed, were they? Anyhow, there wasn't anything for it. This was what he'd come for, this windmill. So it was into the arena, and the best of luck!

It was probably like any farmer's yard, Ritchie decided: old bits of engines, odds and ends of machinery and wheels and empty oil drums that might come in useful, with a couple of useful buildings next to the mill – a corrugated shack on one side and some sort of a garage on the other. The windmill society man would have wanted all this tidied, of course: but this was for real, the building was still serving some purpose. Up close, it took a good stretch of the imagination to make it into an olde worlde teapot. But this was the place all right, the angle of those sails told him that, as certain as a signature.

Now all he needed to know was, did the owner know of Billy Collins and his business? And if he did, where did the man hang out. Failing that, did he know who might? So close now to what could be a moment of truth, Ritchie felt the turn of nervousness inside; but a steadying hand to the camera case gave a thought of his father still dying till the right person was found, and his heart seemed to swell with fighting blood.

He made no secret of being there. He was on business. Besides, a yapping dog – some mongrel, not an alsatian – had suddenly come scrabbling round from the side on a thin rope, followed fast by a young woman, all eyes and cocked head.

"Yes? Can I help you?" She quietened the dog with a hand on its collar and stood frowning in the sun at Ritchie: jeans, twill shirt, long hair: an officer's daughter if ever he saw one.

"I wondered...er...could I have a word with the owner? Please?"

"Yes, that's me. Well, one of them." She was being very businesslike. And suspicious.

"It's about souv...." But Ritchie never got out the rest. The other owner had emerged, the man. He came through the door of the windmill itself and stood frowning at Ritchie, too: much older than his partner, older than Ritchie's dad. And Dick Collins' brother without the shadow of any doubt. Ritchie had gone cold, except where a sudden rash of sweat prickled round the backs of his legs, and he could only stare into the same grey eyes, at the face which would sharpen with the family nose if you put a red helmet over the head. There was less hair on the head and more breadth to the shoulders; he was straggly and untidy; but this man was his uncle, he was absolutely sure of that.

114

The man was saying something to him. Staring hard, as if letting the dog loose could be a possibility.

"Sorry?"

"I asked you if you wanted something. This place isn't open to the public." But he wasn't turning to go, the way people do when they're casually waving you off. He had his hands in the back pockets of his jeans, his weight on one foot, and he was making sure Ritchie went.

The search was over. Already.

"I'm not the public. I'm Ritchie Collins – Dick Collins' son."

The girl shot a look at the man; but the man's eyes stayed on Ritchie. "Dunno what you're on about. That doesn't mean nothing to me." His voice came from the same throaty place Dick's did, but it was rougher; and by the way he stood Ritchie could see he'd never come to attention in his life. He tried not to blink. It was like confronting the old dragon at the pub, looking into that unfriendly stare.

From somewhere behind him, Ritchie heard the throttle and whooping of a couple of motorbike hill-billies, roaring up the private road, shouting and laughing. He took a step nearer to the man. "Can I talk to you? Please! I've got to explain..."

But the revving was louder now as the bikes went round the windmill mound on what could have been a favourite moto-cross track: and Billy Collins had to shout. "Bugger it! Come in here, then. But I'm telling you, son, you've got this all wrong."

Ritchie nodded his thanks, just waited to see the girl take a firm hand on the dog, and followed the man towards the door.

"But only for a minute, where we can hear ourselves think." He stopped and watched Ritchie go past; could almost paint a hateful picture of him, Ritchie thought, from the hardness of the stare.

It was an unwelcoming room, the base of the windmill: it had a rough concrete floor covered in grotty mats, and stacks of boxes all over the place printed with wine glasses showing THIS WAY UP; while everything else was the cheap three-sailed windmills he'd seen before: plates, cups, saucers, salt and pepper pots. And prints of the pictures at Gran Collins, all in various sizes. What small windows it had were covered in heavy cobwebs and iron bars; and when the door was closed it would be firm against the world with slotted steel. Billy Collins was making the windmill gimmick pay, that was for sure.

"Now who do you say you reckon I am?"

The man was leaning back against a crate of crockery, his arms folded and wearing what Des Banks called the 'innocent villain' smile; that old East End look put on by every actor who ever played a crook. And just as easily seen-through. Ritchie took a breath. "Billy Collins. You're Billy Collins, my dad's brother. You could *be* him, my dad." Ritchie's boldness came from *knowing*.

But the man was shaking his head, more innocent than ever. "Listen to me, son, I haven't got a brother. Sorry, but I haven't. So what do you say to that?"

Ritchie kept on looking at him. A lifetime's experience had taught him when his dad was lying, and he could see the same look here: something about his mouth which couldn't quite close.

"Yeah, he says that, too, that not-having-a-brother-stuff. But I've been over to The Street. Hornchurch Elms. I've seen your windmill pictures on the wall, and your teapot on the shelf and your necklace round the old lady's neck. And you're him. I know it, so I don't know why you're saying no."

The head shaking came back, spilling out scorn. "Do you know, son, we can't find a place for the dog to crap some Saturdays, there's so many artists out there. Bloody windmill with three sails! An' we sell this stuff all over the place. I'd be put out if some old girl *didn't* have one round her neck!"

The young woman came in now, started taking cups from

one crate and packing them into another in a showy sort of way: just to be there, Ritchie reckoned, because that hadn't been what she was doing when he'd arrived: she'd come from round the back. Something funny was going on. But nothing like the funny business of two brothers who both said they hadn't got a brother...

"Well, what is your name, then? If it isn't Billy Collins?" Ritchie suddenly sounded more like a policeman, didn't know where this boldness was coming from. Perhaps it was fear for his dad. Or stubborness: he'd got plenty of that from his mum. But what had suddenly dawned on him was that the motorbike revving had gone away, and now they were all alone in this remote spot... Who knew what terrible things this ex-brother had done...the man his parents didn't want to own...?

"Listen, I don't have to answer your questions, son. I've told you I'm not your bloody uncle, so just accept what I'm saying, eh? Now clear off out of it 'fore I start losing my rag..." He took a step towards Ritchie. But somehow his eyes weren't cold enough. And Ritchie stood his ground.

"All right. You tell me your name and I'll go. Show us one of your papers." Ritchie waved vaguely at the documents which were sticking out of various boxes and bulldog-gripped on a wall. "You've got to have it printed somewhere."

Now the man did get angry. He turned away and then roared round in some sort of disbelief. "I don't believe I'm hearing this! I don't believe it! Listen, son, I'll tell you what I bloody *will* do. I'll phone the law, that's what. Bear me out, Lyn – I've not laid a finger on him. The law can sort this one out."

His voice could easily have been Ritchie's dad when he was having a go. And like that other man of real action, he made a sudden move to keep his word. By the door, in the first of the room's many corners, a steep and open flight of steps went up to the floor above. With a loud creak of boards he ran up; the girl standing still as if struck and

Ritchie staring up at the empty rectangle till the ping of the telephone was heard. So Billy Collins wasn't bluffing – at least, not over phoning the law.

"I know for certain it's him," Ritchie said weakly. "He's the spit of my dad. I'm not doing this for fun, you know. It is important." He looked at her face, not a lot older than Lucy's and the sort, somehow, who seemed as if she might understand. "It's a matter of life and death."

But she said nothing, looked up to the aperture in the ceiling through which the low murmur of the man's voice could be heard, and quietly she began burying plates in straw again. Billy's girl-friend, she had to be: and about as confused over all this as he was.

Ritchie's heart was thumping. He'd never been arrested before, wasn't the sort who'd ever seen himself with a re-mote chance of being arrested. But he could picture June's face when she was told: he could see her hitting the ceiling at his pig-headedness leading to this. Imagine them phoning her at Barry August to tell her he was under arrest down here!

The man's feet and legs led the way back down the stairs. "Son, you've got about ten minutes, I reckon. I'm not stop-ping you if you wanna get off..." He put up his hands like the footballer who hasn't committed the foul, nodded his head at the door. "I'm not a vindictive man, but I've had it just about up to here..."

And now Ritchie was caught between going and staying. Even his feet in their trainers were set awkward on the floor as the two sides of his mind tried to come to a decision. The man was giving him a chance to go: but if he stayed could he somehow explain the full strength of how things were, and get to the truth? Had the man been bluffing, only pretending to call the police? Or if he hadn't been bluffing and the police came, could being arrested somehow affect the end of his dad's career and his pension for next year?

"All right. I'm going. But I...definitely...know who you are."

118

"And you are well wrong, I keep telling you!"

The man was at the foot of the steps, the girl was at the crate, Ritchie was in the middle and just about to shift when the moment was suddenly broken by the roar of the hill-billies coming back on their bikes. But now their voices were as raucous as their machines, and something hard clanged on the corrugated iron of the outhouse: a stone thrown up from a wheel - or just thrown. It made the dog yap. It was the man who moved. He swore and went running out to them. "Oi! Come here! Just come here you little toe-rags! If I get hold of one of you...!" His voice was lost in a roar of exhaust and foul insult.

And yet in all his anger, Ritchie noticed, he didn't shout that the police were coming! Now his own nervous uncertainty returned, and with it that bladder pressure he'd forgotten.

"I know I'm being awkward," he told the girl in as reasonable a voice as he could, "and I'm clearing off, I really am, but do you think I could use your lavatory before I go?"

She looked at him and he smiled, opened his hands to show that he wasn't armed, or anything.

"Hang on. Wait till...my partner comes back."

"If he's quick. I don't reckon I can wait for long. Sorry."

"Oh, come on!" She threw a frustrated handful of straw at the crate, went to the door, looked out, looked back: wanted to keep an eye on Ritchie and also on the man who seemed to have gone out of sight. "Stay there, then. Right there." She pointed to the mat Ritchie was on, well away from any papers he might grab a look at, put her head out of the door, then her body, just a foot left behind. And then she'd gone for a second, calling the man without using a name. "Er – are you there? Where are you? I want you here a minute."

The dog's yapping had stopped; so Billy was a little way away. And right now the girl was out of sight. Quickly, for he hadn't meant to, Ritchie looked about. Which piece to grab? He'd only got a few seconds. Which piece of paper to pick up first? If he could wave the evidence of Billy Collins' name under his nose, wouldn't he *have* to let him stop and talk? The nearest! Leaning over to one of the crates Ritchie grabbed out a handful of dockets, riffled and tore at the thin sheets. But they were all long numbers and computer talk. He stuffed them back. Where else then? Bewildered, he twisted about. Did people have their names written up on their phones? Private owners? Ritchie couldn't remember, he'd only ever been army in an army flat. But almost without a conscious thought now, Ritchie dived for the stairs. This *was* Billy Collins, he knew it. And there had to be some sort of proof up here. Four-footed and fast Ritchie climbed up and pushed his head through the hole to the floor above. Rush mats, wooden floor, easy chairs, big television, just one crate spilling shredded paper – and there, on a low glass table, the telephone. From down outside he heard the voices coming back round the building, an angry edge to the man's: "You left him *where*?" as Ritchie's eyes scanned the phone. He grabbed at it, almost failed to see the information on it in the panic of looking. But, yes? No! just the number as far as he could see, under the receiver, on the same model that they had at home, the number partially hidden till you lifted it. No name: but what about getting the number? Who knew how that might come in useful...

*The same Ambassador phone as the one at home!* With all the buttons! Suddenly something had clicked in his head. With that same button on the bottom right! *LR*. Last number redial. His mother's clever trick.

The door went, downstairs: it slammed, trapping him. "Where? Where?" And the thump of hands and feet were coming up the stairs.

All caution thrown, Ritchie pressed the receiver to his ear, pushed the button: stared like a rabbit at the hole in the floor as the man's head came through. Red, angry. "What the...!" Up he came; big and frightening, while a million connections got made inside the machine. So *had* Billy Collins phoned the law? *Were* they on their way?

120

"Give that bloody thing here!"

But Ritchie held on. Pressed the thing hard to him as if it would mark his head for ever. And, "Barry August Products," his mother's voice bore into him, a fraction before the phone was ripped away.

"So you're the soldier-boy's son!" Billy Collins shovelled it at him, heaped with scorn. "Well, I've still got sod all to say to you."

Ritchie was sitting down now, had been allowed to use the small modern bathroom on the top floor and been brought down to sit and be told how nothing had changed. The girl, Lyn, was in the other chair doing more staring at the floor than anywhere else; but Billy Collins was putting on a show of real anger, and Ritchie in his bewilderment was working up a real anger, too. This man had actually been on to his mother; they'd talked together about it before he'd tried to see him off – and all the time he could be standing there with the right bone marrow to save his brother's life.

"He's very ill! He could die! How can anyone say no to helping their own brother..?"

"You got a brother, have you? You know what it feels like?" Billy Collins' face had taken on a cynical look.

"No..."

"So you must know what it feels like *not* to have a brother. Well, my son, that's what it feels like for me..."

Ritchie felt his own face twisting up at the hatred of the man. What the hell was going on – what the hell *had* gone on – to leave Dick and Billy Collins denying the other one even existed? And where did his mother fit into all this? *He'd been phoning her*, for Crissake!

"You've been onto my mum. You know what I'm saying's right. Has she told you about the sisters not matching – or haven't you got those, either?"

"Oh, don't come the little soldier here, son. Leave out doing your *duty*, please!" His voice was hoarse when he was

121

loud, but still strong, like a market trader's, or a sergeant major's. "You wanna say anything, you go home and say it to your mum. She's the one for you to talk to. But don't come here again, and don't ask me no more stupid questions." It was like being back at Gran Collins', that same cold hate.

"Look, his best chance is with a matched donor who's a brother or a sister. You might not be any good – but, please, it's worth a chance, isn't it? Five minutes, it takes, the test. And I bet they'll do it local, if you want." Ritchie tried to swallow his anger, forget his bewilderment and put on the most helpful and appealing face he could find.

"Look, get lost, boy. Just leave it out, will you?" Billy Collins was getting loud again. "You go an' try all this somewhere else, because I wouldn't climb those stairs to save his life!"

"*Billy!*" Lyn jumped up. "There's no need for that."

At which Billy turned, and snorted. "I'll decide what there's need for and what there isn't!" He swung back at Ritchie. "No, you do your *duty*, sonny-boy, and get back on that bus, and tell June Collins to keep on looking somewhere else. How many times do I have to say it? I won't come for her an' I won't fall for a trick like sending you! Got it clear?" He came over and shook the back of the chair, the way his father used to do when Ritchie had defied an order to bed.

Ritchie obeyed. He got up, and with a last look at Lyn, who was back to staring at the floor, took a defeated drop down through the floor and out of the three-sailed windmill. Kicking at stones, swearing at the incessant squawk of sea birds, he followed the distant sound of motorbikes back to his bus; not only beaten but desperately worried at what sort of game his mother was playing.

If they reckon it's better to travel hopefully than to arrive, what does going home in that sort of defeat amount to? Ritchie's head banged on the bus window as the wheels hit some bumps; and hopelessly he let the head-banging happen. Because it *was* all so hopeless. There was nothing else in the world he could do now, was there? You couldn't take a man to court and make him be tested for a transplant.

The afternoon sun lit the grime on the window, its late heat reminding Ritchie of his threat to drown his sorrows in a drink. But he'd save up his thirst till he was back in Thames Reach, give a lager top billing all the way home, just to stop him going crazy over all this bad Collins blood.

But patience has its limits. He more or less fell out of the train at Thames Reach Station and straight in through the doors of *The Bold Hussar*, money ready in his hand. He didn't worry too much about not being served. He'd done this at Christmas with Sunil and Tony and no-one had looked at him then. Anyhow, he felt old enough – about a hundred and fifty if anyone wanted to know, with enough bad experiences behind him to last a good hundred and fifty more. *Eighteen?* How could age on its own be the way they measured maturity?

And there wasn't any bother. If it had been hot down on the coast it was hotter still in London, and all the Town Hall people seemed to have suddenly found the need to murder beer. The place was packed, and it was his hand with the money that got to the bar, half a carpet away as he mouthed for his drink.

And God, it went down well. It had him standing against the flock on the wall as relaxed as all the council clerks; one of the well-deserving at the end of a sticky day. But he'd forgotten that he hadn't eaten, that what was filling his stomach now was the first thing since breakfast. Buoyed by the first, a foot beginning to tap in time to the juke box, he went to the bar for another; slid his glass under the nose of the barman and side-tipped his money onto the polish. Lovely! It was only when he was halfway down through this second that he really began to understand what he was doing; that like a lot in there he was only delaying the going home... And he was three sips into his third pint before he could taste the failure as well as the drink. Real bitter! His vision was as blurred as watering eyes, and suddenly all he wanted was a fierce cuddle and a long, long cry. Except for the stares, he would never have finished the glass; but when he had, he fixed the door as his target and made for it, only grim determination holding back the tears. Shouldering, swaying as if his trainer laces were tied together, he pushed out in to the evening sun.

The evening sun – which seemed to want to show everyone what strength it had left; which didn't so much hit him as weigh on him – forced his stare down at a pavement which was suddenly there in great detail, as if his brain couldn't decide between what was important to see and what was not. All at once the way a lamp post fitted into the paving was as interesting as the kerb at a road crossing, an ant as sharp as another pedestrian. But still roaring with the drink in Ritchie's brain were those deep waves of defeat: and he saw them all in detail, too. Finding Billy Collins and being seen off like that, staring into the same hateful face as he'd met at Hornchurch Elms, being in the same room as someone who wouldn't lift a finger to save a life, a brother's life! – it was the most horrible thing that had ever happened to him. He hated the man – and he hated himself for not shouting it out.

The selfish bastard! Ritchie swayed into a privet hedge, brought up a pint's worth of wind from somewhere deep in his soul. And he went on swearing from the station to the Common, using every word he knew; only nearer his home, coming into the army estate, the words of the swearing lost their meaning and they just ran together from his mouth in a stream of sound – an anguish standing in for tears. Just one prickle in the eye and he'd let go, he knew, blurring him even more, having him falling all over the place. So he just about held on: but he was crying all right, from a depth too profound for any tears.

It was all over, then – what had been driving him. His dad might live or he might die: but this best chance he'd been going for was over.

Ritchie spat at a tree which had attacked him, and as he came reeling off it, he looked up at the bright sky and swore into the eye of God.

"Ritchie! Ritch! You all right, Ritch?"

Ritchie wiped his mouth, twisted himself straight, turned to where the voice had come from. It was Sadie. He hadn't realised he was passing her house but there she was in the garden, dropping someone's cat. And now she was running over, in a Hong Kong singlet and short shorts, her dark hair swaying and catching the sun.

Ritchie saw her through each eye, separately.

"You look terrible! Where've you been?"

"Southend. The windmill..." Close up, she came together.

"Did you find him?"

"Yeah, but..."

They were going indoors. She had his hand and was pulling him into the cool.

"Ritch, you look ill. I'll get you a drink."

He stopped on the doorstep, pulled back. He was drunk. Drunk, he was, and he couldn't go in there with her dad.

"Come on. They're out. Have a Coke. You need something..."

The next he knew he was on her settee, half lying, half sitting, propped into its corner like some big doll. And then she was there with the Coke on a small table, and sitting next to him, being kind: a shoulder to cry on.

And that was too much. He could fight against everything except kindness: Billy Collins, the Essex gran, his mum and dad and Pearson's gang: but kindness was too much. Sympathy, soft words and that smooth, shining shoulder... And giving way, feeling himself go, he nestled against it and began to sob, wetting her as she put an arm round to comfort him.

"Ritchie, my poor Ritchie. You can cry. Please cry."

But almost at once, like a cuddled baby searching with its mouth, instead of crying he was kissing; clutching at her,

125

holding her tight as if he were hanging over some precipice, kissing out his tears till his racking, sobbing sadness was a press on her mouth which hardly let her breathe. And not being pushed away, head stupid with the drink, his feet off the ground and his spirits lifting at this soft comfort, he began to lose his sense of limits. It felt as if Sadie was him and he was Sadie. His head was back and light as a balloon and he couldn't summon a swallow as he rumpled the singlet up. "Christ!" his throat said. "Oh, God..." He thought he'd burst with this feeling. One touch and he'd hit the stars, go through them: and, instead of being embarrassed in his jeans, he pulled himself round and pushed against her as if he had some contest to win.

"I'm your friend, Ritch. Ritchie..." Her hands were at the back of his neck holding onto him like some post in a rough sea. But Ritchie had no anchor, either. He just wasn't ever going to stop; Sadie, Lucy, whoever this was. And with a clumsy expertise from his fantasies he began to go too far.

"No, Ritchie, don't do that..."

But he took no notice. His head was swimming, his body was in crisis and he wouldn't stop. She was fighting his hands with hers.

"No, Ritch! Please! Please don't spoil..."

He was stronger, though, and he didn't care. She'd soon give up. "Sadie, Sadie, yes..." Soft words, strong arms.

And the front door banged shut.

"Sadie?" Mrs O'Connell shouted.

Springing back in a flurry of limbs, Sadie pulled herself together like someone on the end of an electric wire. While Ritchie, gone too far, swore in his grovelling panic to sit in a chair and try to cross his legs.

"You in here, pet?"

Sadie had thrown herself into an armchair a million miles from him. "Hi, Mum. All right? Oh, this is Ritchie. You've never met Ritchie, have you?"

Ritchie couldn't get up. "'Lo!" He gave a doubled over wave from the settee. Suddenly sober, he saw that Mrs

126

O'Connell was a small Chinese woman in a nurse's uniform. She was smiling, and if she thought there was anything up she wasn't showing it; not the way Ritchie's mother would have done.

"Oh," she said, suddenly serious. "You're the boy with the father."

"Yeah." Now Ritchie remembered. He was the boy with the father: the sick father he hadn't been able to help.

"Have you been lucky yet?"

"No. No luck. No luck at all . . ."

Mrs O'Connell frowned, looked from one to the other. "O.K. I'll leave you to it," she said. "Tea in a bit, Sadie, if your friend wants to stay."

She went out to get it, but Ritchie had already measured the steps from his seat to the front door. Suddenly he was off the settee and springing for it.

"I'm sorry, Sayd," he croaked. "See you . . ." And he ran. But he wouldn't see her, he knew; not if she saw him first. He ran out of her house and he legged it away fast with his head down, to a quiet spot he knew on the Common – with insects and with aeroplanes; but, most of all, with a drying sun for his body, and for all his tears.

# CHAPTER EIGHT

It was like the cat with the canary out of its cage at home. Ritchie had never flown so wild and June was clawing at him with every sharp talon. Forget the stink of drink and what he'd done at Sadie's, she was waiting to break his wings for what he'd done at Southend, for finding the person she'd been keeping secret. It was all fur and feathers flying in a cage of guilt.

"How dare you! How dare you run down there behind my back?"

"You knew him! You knew where he was an' you conned me you didn't! He had your rotten *phone number!*" He hadn't been in the door five seconds and already he had reached the bottom line, his voice thick in his throat.

"You disbelieving little Judas! What the hell do you think's going on?" She'd snapped the plastic jewellery off her ears and thrown it into a chair. Now she faced him, both hands ready to grab at his head. "Of course I'd tried! Of course I'd bloody tried!" She started swiping at him. "May gave me his number, that was all! If there was a better chance for my husband, do you think I wouldn't have tried it?" she screeched. "Are you so *stupid?*" And in her anger she got hold of him, grabbed his hair and shook his head by it. "Who says you're the only one, eh? What gives you that right?" With her free hand she hit him, teeth bared, wanting to hurt.

"Oi!" And at first he let her, as if his guilt at what had happened with the girl made it right for him to take some punishment. So his resistance was token, half an arm up. But the attack was not token; it was real and it was uncontrolled, the same as the words.

"Big man! Big conscience! Making up for the time when your mind was filled with that girl!" Another clumping blow at his head. "All...guilty...for not having your dad top of your thoughts! I know you!" And she jerked a painful pull down at his hair which had to have him going with it.

"No!" That wasn't fair! True but not fair, and it cut and hurt. And she was hurting his head. The tears in his eyes were of pain now. Going with the pull, running with it to lessen the pain, he pushed against her until she fell, and suddenly they were rolling, fighting, mouthing hate at each other face to face on the carpet. "Not true. That's...not... true!"

"Ritchie!" she fought him like Sadie had before. "You're mad! You've gone mad!" He'd overcome her with his strength till she could only scream up at him. But she'd really wanted to hurt him with a hate of the family sort. And he did begin to hurt where he was tender, and in another wallow of misery at everything, "Don't you say that to me!" he started sobbing. He got up and fled behind the flimsy lock of the bathroom: spared himself the awful sight of a woman picking herself up off the floor, but imagining it; and finding that he could only squeeze out more tears; not sympathy.

Ages later, when his red, knuckled face was a familiar misery in the mirror, a knock came at the bathroom door.

"I've made some coffee." The voice was straight: no clue in it as to whether this might one day be reported to his father. "Do you want some?"

He wanted to say no. He wanted not to be there, to be a thousand miles away on his own. Or, better, he wanted to be dead: right now his dad could be the lucky one...

"Yeah, all right."

"On the table, then."

Cautiously, head down to hide his face, he came out. But they managed to ignore each other's looks.

"How did you...know where he was?" Ritchie asked her.

June looked into the depth of her black coffee. "I didn't know where he was. Only the phone number. May told me..."

"Not the gran?"

"No." And June sipped at the coffee, although it was too hot.

"You knew he had one, then? A brother? You knew him, back then..."

"Not a lot." She took another scalding sip. "So what did he say?"

"What about?"

June sighed, and broke it off, like a teacher, as if she wouldn't let herself be irritated with Ritchie again. "About anything. About not wanting to be a donor, what do you think?"

Ritchie stared at the table top. "He just said no way. What he must've said to you. Said he hadn't *got* a brother, you know, all that stuff, same as Dad. Didn't want to know. He said you're the one to talk to. An' he told me to clear off..."

June said nothing.

"But why did he phone you? Why did he have your number at Barry August...?"

"Oh, there's no mystery about that." Now she looked him in the eye. "For if he changed his mind." She widened her hands round the mug. "Ritchie, I've left all the doors open, believe me..."

"All right, but what did he say on the phone when I was there?"

And now the coffee was finished, no more to drink. June put the cup down slowly onto its mat. "He swore at me for using you. He thought I'd sent you, to do a persuasion job where I couldn't..." She shrugged. "He's a peculiar man; they're a very funny family..." She breathed in and out deeply again, still trembling with the shock of their awful fight.

"You're not coming in to see your father tonight. I'll

130

think of something to say: he can't see you like that, not even in a mask; not even under a police blanket..."

There was a time when Ritchie would have smiled. But things had changed: the old tricks wouldn't work any more.

"So what went wrong with them two? Why *do* they hate each other's guts?"

June scooped up the coffee mugs, chinked them together hard, moved away towards the kitchen. "Oh, it goes back a long way, I think..." The mugs went into the sink: and then she was back at the door. "But you did your best, Ritchie. And I'm sorry for what I said. Your dad would be proud of you..."

Ritchie looked at her, and then away out of the window. Well, that was something. He *had* tried, hadn't he, for all the right reasons? There was a hell of a lot not to be proud of, though. And was it him or was it her?

But with her congratulation given, she'd turned her back and gone at once, no forgiving hand on his shoulder.

Des Banks was a hand on the shoulder man, someone Ritchie admired. The way he dealt with difficult kids without turning into a sergeant major was really impressive; and if you were lucky enough to have lessons from him, he said things from time to time which stuck with you, and became part of your own thinking.

One of these thoughts applied to 'A' level work. At the start of their course he'd tried to show the difference between the level of the exams they'd done and what they were on about now.

"Just stop taking what we say for granted any more. Other people's minds have got you through so far. From now on the examiners are judging *yours*. Don't read one account of an event, read them all: read wide and go down beneath the surface. And remember, the louder something's said, the less there is to it; think of the politicians. And especially don't take my opinion as gospel. Keep telling yourself, everybody's got an angle..."

131

So what were some of the angles in this business of the brothers? Billy Collins' angle, and his parents' angle, — and the Essex gran's? And why should he accept that there was no more to be done, as one of those loud voices had been telling him? Couldn't someone try to put things right between the two brothers? And if everything had gone off before June had come on the scene, wasn't there one key person who could help to do that?

That big woman over at Hornchurch Elms...

Alone in the flat Ritchie prowled round the rooms and thought about it. What would Des Banks have done in all this: would he have left it? Would his own father have given up right now?

The answer was obvious. It came back at him from every hard-won regimental trophy he prowled past. No! He had to go on. He had to go back to the Essex gran.

Which was not easy. Physically, it was. Getting out and onto a 108 gave him no trouble. He was still on half-term and the day was his own, his mother couldn't lock him up and he was too old to be taken to work with her. Inside him, though, it was a killer. The last time he'd done this same trip had been with Sadie, when she'd given him the guts to see it through. But on the bus ride now, whether he was alone on a seat or with someone's shopping crowding him against the window, he kept coming over in a cold clam of shame at what he'd done the day before at Sadie's house. He kept hearing her voice pleading, kept seeing her face with its look of love turn to disgust at what he'd tried to do.

No way to prepare for the hell he'd got coming today... He got so caught up with the thoughts which kept coming that he almost missed the Green Line stop to get off. But this was the crossroads; he was there — and too soon, he thought. He hadn't had time to wind himself up and now he had this dragon to face...

It was sunny again, like the day before in Southend: and by the time he got to The Street, the pub garden was open

132

and metal tables and bright umbrellas gave the pretence of a good English summer. Playing it cagily, that's where Ritchie went, into the safe ground of the garden: eight or eighteen he could have a Coke in there, couldn't he? A couple of salesmen were looking at figures over their half-pints and cheese rolls: otherwise the garden was empty.

Lucky devils doing ordinary things! What on earth had driven him to thinking he could get anything out of Gran Collins? The thoughts he'd had back in the flat had seemed all right there but they were all wrong now he was here. That woman would shrivel him with her first look, let alone one of her loud words. Ritchie tapped his nails on the white metal table and looked around him. They didn't have waiters in pubs, did they? You had to go and get it. He waited for five minutes till one of the salesman went inside for refills: then he went inside himself. His stomach was up in his throat, his throat up in his mouth. But the heavy garden chair had needed a good lift in the longish grass, and that sent him pushing in the door with the macho feel of muscle. Image! It was all image, till it came down to trying to get what you wanted.

And there she was behind the bar, not looking any different to the way she'd looked before: still in her masculine blouse, still all face and flattened hair. The bar was almost empty; just an old man trying to include his dog in things, with the big woman not having any; wouldn't look at what he did with a crisp dunked in stout; kept her eyes on her rinsed glasses.

Until Ritchie walked in. And then the way she looked up at him he thought she'd crack the bar mirror, shout and send him packing. But she didn't even raise her voice. Without a word she ripped the top off a Coke and poured it into a tumbler with ice: she flipped a packet of crisps up onto the bar top: and waving Ritchie to them she faced him square.

"So – you want to know *why*," she told him. "You found him but you don't know why he won't come running to help you." The dog looked up enquiringly. She poured

133

herself a rum. "All right, then, boy," she said. "All right, if your mother won't, I'll have to tell you." And she downed the fiery drink in one gulp.

They were back in the terraced cottage, after the pub's lunchtime opening was over. Ritchie had been sent for a walk; told where to go to pass the time; told to follow The Street all the way out beyond the chapel till he came to Bennett's Farm, and then to make his way slowly back to number twelve.

He'd taken his time. It was a quiet road leading to nowhere and to everywhere; the sort of road running out of the village that people set off along at the start of adventure films. As he'd walked birds had sung in the trees and insects buzzed in the bushes; and he'd remembered something Des Banks had said about some old relative from Vauxhall never seeing a bird's nest till she was eighty. Living in London you didn't know the real country at all – it was only those bits on each side of the motorway – when really it was a terrific sort of place for anyone to grow up, all quiet and peaceful.

It was a long road and not much had passed him on it. He'd admired the houses set back in their own patch of land and surrounded by fields, walked down the steep road to Bennett's Farm and back up again.

Now she made him a cup of tea in her tidy formica kitchen, sat in her slacks at the angle of the stairs which led to the bedroom. She nodded at another windmill picture on the wall, this one a water-colour.

"Not bad, is he, with a paint brush? You good at art, are you, boy?"

Ritchie looked at that special windmill again: it was a bit romantic, having seen the real thing. "Not so's you'd notice," he said.

The moments passed. A clock on the wall came into step with the drip of a tap and had time to go out again before Gran Collins got up and threw her tea grouts in the sink, screwed the tap off.

"So where did you walk? Where I told you?"

"Yeah, I think so. Along past the chapel, down the dip to that farm and then back again."

"Good. Keep that in your head. Now have a look up here." She pulled herself at the stairs, started to lead the way: suddenly stopped at the angle where she'd been sitting and turned back to him. "You do want to know, don't you?" Ritchie nodded. His face had never been so straight, so serious; not even with the news of his dad. "Come along then, boy. An' mind your head." Ducking, she led him up to the small landing, which was a narrow, sloping floor lit only by the open door of the bedroom facing him. To his left was another, smaller door which opened on to a poky bathroom with a w.c.

"Country style, this house is. Farm labourer's. Forget that luxury." She rapped her fist on the partition which made the bathroom. "All one room, this was, for a whole family. Big bed for Mum and Dad, one not-so-big for the boys and another for the girls. Eh?" She surveyed it, as if she were remembering the night lights and staggered bed-times. But now there was just the one bed and it was single, with no more around it that was personal than there was downstairs. A cheap alarm, a small chest with a magazine on it, a walnut wardrobe, plain wallpaper, and two cornflake-packet pictures. The room was lit from one small window at the front and a bulb without a shade. Anyone could have lived there. And no-one.

"Privy was out the back and we washed in the kitchen sink," she said. "An' we reckon we had it good compared to your slums."

Ritchie went on staring into the room. What a sad old place. What a choker for his dad, living here.

"Now come back down an' I'll make some sense of it for you." Ritchie let her pass and followed. "See, I know you found your way to Southend, boy; he phoned me. And when I saw you in *The Wheatsheaf* I knew..." She led the way through, still talking. "She hasn't told you, has she?"

135

Ritchie didn't answer; didn't know what to say for the moment, and the big woman spun round in the living room doorway to catch his face. "No, she hasn't," she said, "or why would you be wasting my time?"

But Ritchie didn't dare to answer. It was all going to come, and this wasn't the time for him to talk. Not immediately, nor at the start when she'd sat him down, nor at the end when she'd done. Like the old saying, there was no answer to all that.

"Right, there's four children: two boys an' two girls, an' a father away at sea – till his line packed up. Roof over their heads, going to school regular, growing up and finding their feet. Nothing special; nothing wrong; Billy, the eldest; then Eileen and May; and Dick who came last – the afterthought, one long leave in a dock strike..." She said it all very matter-of-fact, hands across her middle, fingers locked, not a hint of humour and hardly any rise in her voice, as if she were only testing for sound. "Eileen and May marry and off, no need to go into that. Billy takes himself a girl-friend, normal run of things, fully expected – a Dagenham girl he met at Fords, nothing special to look at, always well-spoken enough to me..."

Ritchie's back was straight; he tried to show her by sitting up how he respected her telling her family history.

"They're going strong, stay downstairs courting when we've gone up, all the old story; on the list for a council place at Dagenham, hinting about one of the beds and any spare sticks of furniture. While the afterthought, your father, is jumping around not knowing whether to be a fireman or a motor mechanic: but he fancies the cars and gets asked to a proper interview on New Year's Eve. Fords. Real engineering, using his City and Guilds... Goes off to it on his motorbike."

Gran Collins' eyes were still fixed above Ritchie's head; and with the matter-of-fact way she was telling it, he wondered how often the woman had gone over this story in her head, sitting there in that chair, waiting for some grandchild

136

who had to know.

"Billy and his father and me go off in the Prefect for a New Year drink at Oldchurch with May. That's where she's living. And it's started to snow, and Billy's not sure whether the girl-friend's coming or not; no blessed phones then; so we leave a key under the flower pot in case. Billy has to drive us, doesn't want to, but he's all for pleasing his father. And he leaves the Martini out for the girl, being New Year." Gran Collins' fingers had unlocked themselves and she waved at the door for the flowerpot, at the kitchen for the Martini. "But the snow keeps on. Fine stuff. 'Little snow, big snow' and it keeps on blessed coming down, and coming down..."

Already Ritchie was buzzing ahead. So what had happened next to cause all the trouble? Had his dad come back and drunk all the Martini? Had he *run over the girl-friend on the road?* Oh, God!

And as he thought it, a coldness held his spine: a chill which spread to freeze his face and his hands. And even worse, as he looked at Gran Collins she was no longer staring into the distance above his head but into his eyes; and she was nodding.

"There's no quick way back from May's without a slope like that one this side of Bennett's Farm. The white stuff keeps coming on down while we're drinking, and when we look out...it's too blessed late. The lanes are closed and there's no rescue vehicles getting up Bennett's Hill for hours. The only way back is all round the world..."

Ritchie was gripping his chair and with the first chill gone was prickling with a nervous sweat. Come on! What was it? Something terrible was coming and he wanted to know it, quick.

"An' while the snow's starting to fall your father isn't getting his job; he's slapped in the face, hard. They interview him, test him, look at his papers, and tell him there and then. Not good enough. No thanks, and there's the door, son; on your motorbike... His first real disappointment, and the fool can't take it."

Ritchie's shoulders were knotted like in an old tight jacket. He tried to stretch them. Come on! Get the girl-friend on the road and get her run over! He just couldn't take this holding out...

"All the time, the girl-friend's come and she's here, downing our Martini. And in he comes cold, the bottom out of his world, after a few doses of something stronger... So he lays into the Scotch, and the girl-friend lays into more Martini to keep him company, and she tries to cheer him up, to *console* him..."

Ritchie swallowed hard. Her voice had been very matter-of-fact until then; but she gave that word 'console' all the old acid in the world.

"All cut off, desert island stuff, one drink turns to two drinks turn to three; and the mucky little tykes start to celebrate New Year by consoling one another a bit more besides...and on the fine old excuse of looking out over the fields to welcome us, up the stairs they go..."

Without knowing it at first, Ritchie had closed his eyes: he couldn't face his gran for the moment. But what he wanted to be able to close most were his ears: because the last thing on earth he wanted to hear was the name of that girl-friend. He knew it. But he never ever wanted it confirmed.

It was June Fielding. His mother. And now he knew why he had no relations...

Gran Collins was nodding. "Yes, not stupid are you, boy? You're way ahead of me. Course, it took some time, all of it. Getting drunk enough, and us coming back round the long way on the main roads: leaving the car and walking back from Bennett's Farm. And there's just the one room up there, remember; and the stairs come down into the kitchen. So, no excuses. None expected, and none given, bar the drink..."

Wiping his hands on his trousers, Ritchie stood up. He wanted to get into the open air, away from rooms and pictures and furniture, away from *people*: he wanted to be where he didn't have to put on a face for anyone, be it sympathy or disgust. He wanted to think...

"You tell me, boy — is there a name for hate between brothers? If there is, I'm not clever enough to know it. But I know the meaning, all right. Yes, I do know the meaning of that..."

Probably the hardest thing that Ritchie had ever tried to do was look at his mother through different eyes while pretending that they were the same. Having so long to think about things hadn't helped, all that time to wind himself up to walk in on her as if he'd only been over the park with Lucy, while what he was really doing was getting used to the shattering feeling that everything he'd grown up with had fallen apart; he was just like all the kids he knew whose parents split, except that this split was history, and he was one of the splinters. What he'd always thought of as *them*, the three of them, the family, hadn't been them at all but some other triangle with him as an unwanted extra side, probably the result of that drunken night. Worse, he'd found out that the people he'd trusted most all his life hadn't been able to be trusted by others; not even by people like Billy Collins. His dad had done the dirty on his own brother: his mum had cheated on her boy-friend. It left him spinning like an odd-sailed mill in a gale: fast, unbalanced, threatened with disaster.

When he walked into the flat, Ritchie felt like someone walking in on a spy, or on a mole unearthed: she was the same surface person but with a secret depth to her, or with a cover she'd lived with for so long she'd forgotten its beginnings.

She was in the kitchen preparing chicken breasts for the micro-wave on Ward Sixteen. His dad was starting to fancy some food, keeping more down than up these days.

"Chicken tonight. Chicken à la Adjutant. You know what that means? Boneless!"

Trying to be her old self, Ritchie thought: and looking it. In a summer shirt and light matching trousers she looked so much on top, so much as if nothing in the world had gone wrong, that he even started to doubt what the old woman had told him.

And after visiting his dad, it went further away for half an hour, that story of the snowy night. His stomach actually stopped rolling. In the busy hospital ward, with such an incapable-looking man, with the old business of smiles and bulletins and the holding hands in disposable gloves, what had happened all those years before seemed to have been with different people. Because nothing appeared to have changed. This was all still so much the same. What was really important was that there was still no news of a suitable donor. No-one was panicking, of course, but no-one was over the moon with making preparations either: the matter of the transplant put everything back into perspective.

It wasn't until later, nipping home in the Fiat, that something happened to bring what he'd been told back into focus. A new and a sharp focus.

He caught a glimpse of Lucy walking home from the NAAFI, swinging a shopping bag. She was looking good: her hair was piled up today with a yellow ribbon on the top, and she was in long white shorts and a *Mickey Mouse* top. With a catch of his breath he realised that he'd forgotten all about Lucy for the last twenty-four hours, shelved her in all the dramas. And his stomach gave that old uncomfortable lurch: because she seemed so perfectly content without him, all the joys of summer.

But it lurched again, so much more painfully, as they passed the end of Sadie's road. With what he'd lost. With what he suddenly knew he wanted, and he'd lost.

Ideas rarely come in flashes. Not everything was *eureka* for Ritchie: at least, *eureka* wasn't instant very often. Things grew, his thoughts crossed problems like stepping stones cross fierce streams, not always in straight lines, and often

140

with a choice of footings. So it wasn't until he was alone again, in bed, that it gradually dawned.

He knew someone else, didn't he, who'd been disappointed over something and drunk too much, and when he'd found a loving shoulder to cry on, hadn't known when to stop? And someone else who'd only known the way he felt when things had gone too far for others. Him! Ritchie Collins! And if Sadie hadn't been sober and sensible and tried to do the stopping for them both, then wouldn't he have been responsible for something really bad? If one could do it, couldn't two? What if Sadie had lost her head as well?

It got him out of bed, took him to the window where he opened it wider. Too right! And what sort of a moral statue was Billy Collins? Had he led such a life that he couldn't forgive two people like that? Especially after all these years... Couldn't he be brought to see? Couldn't some pleading be done which would get to the man? From someone who could say he knew? Ritchie walked round his room: and in the restless heat of the weather breaking up, he couldn't find any peace in sleep, not for hours. But at least he knew now that one more thing had to be done the next day. One more frightening thing.

Ritchie was starting to feel like one of those travel freaks who go round with books of bus and train numbers in their pockets, marking off the rolling stock and the vehicles they see. He'd have bought a budget pass for the week if he'd known!

But the weather was definitely cooler today: the skies were cloudy and a wind had blown up. And he did know where he was going this time. He even knew what to say to any misery of a Southend bus operator.

In fact she was very pleasant: had a joke with him about coming down a day too late. How wrong could you be? You get ready for aggro and you meet up with a laugh. Wouldn't it just be great if that could happen with Billy Collins?

If the man had even been there, that is. Having wound himself up tight again, only Lyn was there; not even the dog; and neither she nor Ritchie knew quite what to do about that. She'd have liked to show him the gate, that was clear in her face, but she hadn't got Billy's beef, and she hadn't got his anger. While Ritchie definitely wasn't wanting to seem a threat to her. He'd wait, he said: he'd keep out of her way but he'd wait. In the end she sorted it, the way officers' wives usually do. Politely, not directly involved. "You'd better come in and wait for my partner," she said, "but I'm too busy to entertain you."

"Cheers. Will he be long?"

She shrugged. "As long as it takes for a dog to decide to defecate. They make up their own minds about that sort of thing..."

Ritchie had to smile. He remembered how Des Banks had once raised the question of the history no-one could ever know: how the bowel might privately have affected world history. 'I can't see the Archbishop, I'm on the throne.' Discuss.

"Come in, then. It's cold out here."

It had blown up, too. The tufted grass on the bank was being flattened in gusts and the fixed sails of the windmill above him were creaking as if they'd be happier turning again. In the ground floor work-room, Lyn was making up an order: counting dozens of various pieces of windmill crockery out from straw and into tissue, packing them in a divided cardboard box. She found Ritchie a chair without a back while she got on with her work, very aware of being watched.

Give her a pair of jodphurs and you'd have her. Horsey, Ritchie thought. Long hair, long hands, long legs. And definitely young enough to be Billy Collins' daughter. The girl-friend, more his age than his uncle's. He looked at her eyes when she turned: sharp, intelligent – the sort he knew well. And he wondered where she stood in all this. Loyal to Billy, you'd expect that: but might she be open to another young

142

person's point of view if it was put to her about the life-and-death business of a donor for a dad? For a man very much like Billy Collins. .?

But he didn't get a chance to try. Even as his mind was raking up some sort of an opening remark, he heard the roar of them coming: and so did she. And she, by her upper crust swearing, knew just what that could mean; the sound of motorbikes and yells, those yobs on their machines who'd come for a ride on a boring day. There were three of them, judging by the notes and the revs; but one with all the mouth.

"Can I come in, Princess? Save you from old Rumpel-pumple? I got a good ol' bike here. Get up behind me on this, eh?"

"Aar, aar, aar, aar!"

The others gee'd him up and revved, throttled back for their obscenities to be heard. Through the dusty window Ritchie saw the leader nose his wheel against the gate and push his bike inside. The boy had long streaked hair and his helmet was up his left arm. And he was good. One handed, he put the bike into a tight left turn and held it steady while he went round and round the yard, a skill the Red Helmets wouldn't have been ashamed of.

Lyn had put down her packing and was staring out with Ritchie. "They know he's not here. And they get worse. Those other yobs get some sort of a kick from what this one shouts..."

Ritchie looked at the others at the gate. Every so often they looked about them for a sight of Billy Collins coming back: but in a casual way, not too worried. Their main attention, all open-mouthed, was on the next verbal assault from the boy in the yard.

"I'll give you a joy ride any ol' time..." He was smiling widely, circling still, and coming closer to the mill building on his nearer sweeps. And all the time in perfect control of the bike. "Cradle-snatchin' ol' goat, i'nt he? Can he still...?" But he'd nearly gone too far, and the rest of that

143

was lost in a recovering rev.

Lost or not it was getting to Lyn. She had gone very red and her hands were clenched into tight little rocks. Nervously, she swept the hair back off her face and stared on out: just as the leader came up to the wall and peered in close through the window. A frightening closeness: the feeling of invasion.

Which was when Ritchie, his heart thumping hard and his head drained of blood, had to come away from his chair and go to the door. No way being a hero: but because there wasn't any other choice. He couldn't go on cowering in there like some kid behind a parent's leg. The boy's face scowled on in, caught Ritchie and followed him as he pulled the door open and went out into the gusts. He hadn't the first idea what he was going to say: but things just came into your head at times like that in school and around.

Something about bikes might put them off their stroke. Expert to expert sort of thing. Or he might offer this one out, a bit of front. He'd been hurt by Pearson. Being hurt wasn't any big deal when you'd had it the once: it was the thought of it that scared people. Just as long as it was muscle, and there weren't any knives around.

He opened the door. "Here, mate, leave it out, can't you? Give us a chance in here, eh?"

He meant him and Billy and Lyn, and not having all this hassle when the man came back. Not what they seemed to think he meant. Not their warped reading of the situation.

"Oh..." The leader smiled, a bit sheepish, a bit knowing. He looked Ritchie up and down; mainly down; and focussed through the window again at Lyn in there. "Sorry, mate," he said. And, "Good luck to you, son!" And with loud cowboy whoops he led the others away; in slow formation, heads over their shoulders and a lot of invention going on inside them.

Lyn came out to Ritchie. "Thank God for dirty minds," she said.

Lyn told Billy Collins when he got back with the dog. Not

144

what the louts had read into Ritchie being there, but what he'd actually done: gone out to see them off.

"I'm gonna get something done about them," he said. "One dark night, see if I don't." But his eye didn't stay on Ritchie. It was Lyn he was looking at, perhaps seeing where he stood with her against someone so much younger who had done the business...

"I think you owe him a favour," the girl said quietly.

But Billy had a stillness, a way of standing without shifting his feet which was off-putting: and he stood and stared at Ritchie out in the yard; hands on his hips, then arms folded, then hands on his hips again. He hadn't shaved and his stubble was coming through greyer than his hair. He hadn't changed his shirt since Ritchie had been two days before. And he definitely didn't seem to match Lyn at all. All the same, she went over to him now and put her arm very reassuringly around his waist. Billy unwound it, wanted to go on with his sizing up of Ritchie. "So now you know, eh? She told you, did she?" The wind wisped up his hair but he let it blow.

"Not my mum. *Your* mum. Hornchurch Elms; she told me..."

"Oh?" The man frowned as his eyes watered in the stream of air. For the first time now Ritchie was conscious of the background crashing of the sea, of the tide coming up the bank behind the mill.

"And did she tell you all of it, in your search for the truth?"

This man unnerved him, but he stood his own ground. "Yeah, I think so. I dunno. I reckon." How did you know if someone had told you everything they could.

"Do you? You'd better come in, son. Then we can see what you have been told..."

With a sudden movement off his spot, Billy led the way inside and shut the downstairs door firm, took Ritchie up into the living room on the first floor. In a try at conciliation Lyn poured her man a beer and Ritchie a Coke, tapped some white wine for herself. And then she stood by the window, Rapunzel-like, while Ritchie was sat down where Billy could face him.

"What I'm gonna do is, I'm gonna make you the judge," his uncle said. "I'm gonna tell you the strength of it; and then I'm gonna rely on you to say. You want your old man helped: an' I'm not keen to do it. But you done me a favour, today, an' I owe you one: if you honestly reckon your old man deserves it. . ."

Ritchie put his Coke between his feet. His mouth was dry as dust but he'd never manage a swallow without coughing. What was coming now? What *could* be? His uncle knew he'd come back again, knowing. He knew he'd come to have another go. So why wouldn't he say 'yes' to the man helping his dad?

"Let's see what you do know. You know about the snow?"

Ritchie nodded.

"And the big disappointment, and the drink?"

Another nod. "Yeah, she told me all that."

"And you know about your mother being very, very sympathetic to poor little Richard. . ."

Ritchie did swallow now, and nodded again.

"So you reckon you know the score of it; how we came home across the field, Mum, Dad an' me. An' caught 'em up there, testing the springs. . ."

"Please don't be coarse, Billy." Lyn turned in from staring out over the estuary. "It's not necessary."

Billy snorted: came back to Ritchie. "But we all have to take the rough with the smooth, don't we? Which is what your mother settled for, eh?" He took a long drink of his beer, wiped his moustache with a rag. "It was just about all she could do after it had all gone off. . ."

Ritchie frowned. He did know this, didn't he? Or was Billy Collins going into something else. . .? "How did it all go off?" he asked in a quiet voice. "Was it a fight?"

Billy was staring. "Oh there was a fight all right. But it

146

wasn't me. I *wanted* to get at him, but somehow..."

Ritchie had nearly kicked over his Coke: just saved it with a hand. "So, who...?"

The world had gone very quiet.

"My dad. He laid into Dick with his old seaman's tongue, gave him one hell of a roasting. Gave 'em both what they both deserved. And there was Dick as guilty as hell shouting back with all the language under the sun; and the old man pushes him, to get him off out of it, nothing much. And Dick turns round and gives the poor ol' bugger one hell of a swinger, right in the face. Lucky one, but with all of his strength, all of his old Adam anger. An' then he ran, wi' me after him, an' the old lady screamin' blue murders. An' he's off on his motorbike like the little coward he is... Joined the army, had you, never came back: too ashamed to show his face." He looked away from Ritchie, down at the floor. "An' the old boy died of a broken heart, they say..."

There was a silence inside the mill. Lyn had turned back and was watching Billy gulping off his beer, while Ritchie watched the Coke bubbles dying down, took an enormous interest in them. Outside, the sea was crashing and the wind was roaring round, the three sails straining fit to break free. But the sound to break the silence inside was the catch in Billy Collins' voice. "My old dad," he said. "My dear old dad..."

And the tension was broken and throat muscles worked. Glasses were refilled in all their tight hands.

"So what d'you reckon, Judge? Thumbs up or thumbs down? Does he get my marrow, if it fits... Or does such a man get sweet all from me?"

Ritchie looked away at Lyn in the window, saw her silhouetted through her blouse; saw Sadie. Like father, like son: because he hadn't been able to control it, either. A drink and a kiss and he'd lost all sense. And what had he done when he'd got back home? Wrestled with his mother, all guilty; hadn't been far off hurting her, too. What was in them all, these Collinses? What evil? What was this bad

147

blood?

"Well, Judge?"

But Ritchie couldn't answer. And it was Lyn who did it for him.

"You'll do it, Billy. You'll do it because we *can't* be judges. This boy's not God, and neither are you. Doctors save good men and evil and leave God to do the judging. And so must you..."

Billy turned slowly and looked at her.

"Billy, listen – if your dad had been quick enough to duck the punch, you'd have just held your stupid brother's head under a tap and put him to bed..."

Billy went on staring.

"And the man *is* bringing up this boy..." Suddenly the room had gone very, very still; almost in anticipation of what she was going to say next. "Poor kid." She looked at Ritchie, smiled sympathetically at him. "Think of him standing there, wondering which of you is his father..."

# CHAPTER NINE

*Which of them was his father?* The question went right to the root of him like a probing doubt about life itself: all at once it was at the core of everything to do with his very being, like the heart, the blood, the bone marrow inside him; all things taken for granted till the awful doubt was dropped in like some vicious diagnosis. A doubt almost too big, though, to even start thinking about; and Ritchie could shrug it off one moment, then be grabbing at a mirror or staring behind his mother's eyes the next. *Which of them was his father?* Billy hadn't denied he could have been. It was too loud a question to hear, even, or everything in his life had been a lie. Was Ritchie Collins one big con? Was all this illness nothing to do with him? He'd shrug and swallow. Of course it was. So what had really changed?

With June at work, it seemed quite natural for him to walk in on Dick Collins during afternoon visiting. All he hoped was that the man wouldn't start wondering why he hadn't been doing it every day of half-term. Never mind, that wouldn't matter for long. Once he got going, once he made tracks away from motorbikes and started talking about donors and that brother again, he'd soon understand about that! Because Ritchie wasn't letting that go. Whoever he was, he was going to see this through...

But which of them *was* his father? He knew he was June's son, yes: that was for certain. But who else's from those hateful days: the boy-friend's, or the husband's? Was there some test they could do? If not, if there was no way of putting a father's name-tag on him, what other clues did he carry? Who did he look like? Who did he feel like? His stomach rolled for the millionth time with the shock at even having to ask himself such questions.

Now, still in the dark – because how could he throw any light on it? – Ritchie had come to the hospital on his own to lay the bones of it straight. The bit about Billy's intention to be tested for a transplant anyway; somewhere to start from, in letting on how much he knew; the strength of it being that now he did know, Dick's objections to the idea had to be softened. They'd both go mad, him knowing so much, but that was something they'd all got to live with...

Well, that was the theory of it. When he got there Dick Collins was sitting out, working on a racing car, spot-welding a wing with clear cement. And for a few seconds he couldn't let go; there was a short agony of a wait till both hands could be freed and the Williams set on one side. But Ritchie got a father's big smile. Dick was very pleased to see him, and Ritchie was bucked by the sight of a down of hair thickening again on the man's head.

"Hello, Ritch! Got bored with yourself, have you?"

"No..." Shit! All the words he'd had ready had gone out of the window. How was he going to get into this? "Just thought I'd...er, come to see you..."

"Good on you. Glad you did. Mum all right?"

"Yeah. Fine."

"Good..."

So this was it. Motorbike talk or aggravation. And aggravation was what Ritchie had forced himself to come for.

"Actually, er, I've come to...what I think is...could be, like...a bit of good news..."

"Yes?" Dick's face was straight again, just like those times when a late night out was being negotiated.

"Yeah. Only, see, I've..."

But the face being straight wasn't at Ritchie. It was being straight somewhere behind him, at whoever had just come into the ward; the mouth was set, the eyes were frowning. Was it the doctor with an unpleasant drug? Or the Sister in an organising mood...? Ritchie turned round.

150

It was Billy Collins: in a mask and the same plastic apron they all had to wear.

"God, what a pantomime this is! It's worse'n getting in to see someone in Pentonville."

As if horribly fascinated, Dick Collins couldn't take his eyes off his brother. Ritchie looked from one to the other. Did Dick recognise Billy? Or had he changed too much?

"Christ, you don't look too good, do you? What's happened to your hair?"

But Dick was keeping quiet. He didn't turn away, and he didn't send away. Ritchie, though, slid quietly out of his chair and went to find a back seat somewhere. This wasn't in the running order! Billy Collins had given in to Lyn's argument that he come and get tested as soon as possible; but Ritchie hadn't thought for a second that he'd come barging into the ward.

"I've given 'em my sample. And it seemed a bit under-the-counter not to show my face to you as well. That's all. That's all I came for..."

Dick looked across at Ritchie, and back at his brother.

"All right with you, is it?" Billy went on. "I take it you'll have it, if it fits?"

Dick leaned aside and picked up the model Williams: checked that his glueing hadn't slipped, as if to show that whoever came and went, his real life was still in here right now; but his eye ran down the bonnet and lined itself up on Ritchie.

Billy followed the same line round. "The lot, Dick," he said. "The boy knows the lot. And he did the business, that one. He made me come, didn't you, son? A little bit of guts and the old...*tenacity*..."

Ritchie's eyes followed his feet making circles on the lino. But whose tenacity? he wondered for the umpteenth time. Was it Dick who had it, or Billy? *Whose blood was in him?*

Meanwhile, his uncle and his father – or his father and his uncle – began putting together the pieces of a difficult conversation, like two people working on one of the jigsaws

151

Dick was into: trying different bits, moving a few awkward-shaped questions around.

Anyway, couldn't that tenacity have come from June, from his mum, about whom there was no doubt whatsoever? What was it she'd said when they'd had all this out? *"That night I knew who I'd loved all along. And that was the one I stuck with..."*

The brothers went on awkwardly. Ritchie vaguely heard the words 'Southend' and 'young girl' and 'little business': just one or two with the strength to break into his own thoughts. Otherwise he was on his own now. Because suddenly he was certain who his father was, now that the two of them were here together; no paternity test necessary: there'd never really been any question.

It *had* to be the one it had always been, whatever the other possibility might be, whatever June had done with Billy before. With the new hair growing, Dick's face was becoming a different shape again, more the man in the helmet's, the man who all Ritchie's life had never put a wheel wrong till he had leukaemia. Straight as a dye. Trusted. Not some opportunity man, some wheeler and dealer trying to be eighteen. There wasn't any contest. Whatever had gone off all those years ago, and Ritchie understood Dick Collins' record since could not be faulted, not even by a son, and that was saying something. And there was no way all those years could be a fluke.

*Which of them was his father?* Definitely, no contest. His father had to be his father. The one he'd chosen, the one he would choose every time. Ritchie's stomach rolled, and he smiled. Like adopted kids were told to make them feel wanted, Dick being his father wasn't ordinary like any accident of birth. Ritchie Collins had selected him. And not many got the chance to do that...

The test was positive. The *Terasaki* testing plate had revealed the four necessary tissue-typing factors to be present in Billy Collins' white blood cells. He was a match, and the transplant was on, a month or so later when Dick was in full remission and had gained strength back at home. As Ritchie knew it would be, when he'd found the man. The one chance in four. At the windmill with the missing sail...

It was jubilation on the afternoon the news came through. The M.O. shook all their hands, and even the Sister smiled. But June wanted more – champagne – and she was off to get some: and certainly the patient could have a drop at evening visiting...

On their own again for a moment, Ritchie kissed his father's head. He shook his hand, too, and wouldn't let it go; gave him a look which somehow transmitted everything he felt about the man and what had happened all those years before when he'd done the right thing by June Fielding. The knowledge was there, the understanding, the love.

"Good news, eh?" he said. "Good news."

Dick Collins nodded. "All round..." And then there was a pause, and it was the father who was holding on to the hand. "And you'll give your mum a kiss from me, won't you? When you're home. When it's quiet. We've got a long way to go, Ritchie, and I'm never going to do it without her..."

"Yeah, sure..." Ritchie's voice was all choked up. He'd done well up to now, he thought, but now his dad was telling him something about the specialness of his mum: as much as a father can ever tell a son without embarrassment.

Ritchie went then, and left the hospital to it. It was a grey afternoon but there was no way he could face the paperwork of his energy project yet. Anyway, he knew where he'd go. He'd go to pick up the threads of his own life again, find Lucy, go to see the Red Helmets practising, tell them to keep a Suzuki warm for his dad. And with what he thought was a jaunt in his step, he took himself to the end of the road which led to Lucy's flat – and was about to turn into it when he stopped: there on the corner, under a tree. Because something was stopping him from going any further. Something which was only a vague feeling at first, before it became a thought.

He was going the wrong way. His head was taking him to Lucy's, where he'd been telling himself he should go; where the *idea* of love seemed so good. But his feet wanted him to go somewhere else.

His feet? No, the blood thumping in his heart.

He lingered in the shade, under the tree, hoped he hadn't already been seen. And with a sudden decisive twist he crossed the road and ran instead towards Sadie's, where he would risk having his face slapped or the door slammed in his face: but where he would beg her pardon, and somehow try to show her what a nice bloke he could be.

## ACKNOWLEDGMENTS

I should like to gratefully acknowledge the generous help given to me in my research for this book by Dr. N.J. Dodd, the Ipswich Hospital; Colonel J.H. Foxley, Queen Elizabeth Military Hospital; Dr. E.C. Gordon-Smith, Royal Postgraduate Medical School, Hammersmith Hospital; Dr. David James, The Anthony Nolan Laboratories; Warrant Officer Ivor Mason, Team Leader, Royal Artillery Motor Cycle Display Team; Dr. R.H. Phillips, Westminster Hospital; and especially my cousin, Terence Mott, Consultant in the Department of Radiotherapy and Oncology at the Ipswich Hospital, Suffolk, who contributed greatly himself and made the rest of the research possible.

B.J.A.